# A CROSSROADS ADVENTURE

in the World of
## C.J. CHERRYH'S MORGAINE

# THE WITCHFIRES OF LETH

by
Dan Greenberg

TOR

A TOM DOHERTY ASSOCIATES BOOK

# DEDICATION

## Special thanks to Ardyth Gilbertson

THE WITCHFIRES OF LETH

Crossroads Game/novels are published by TOR Books by arrangement with Bill Fawcett and Associates.

First printing: September 1987

A TOR Book

Published by Tom Doherty Associates, Inc.
49 West 24 Street
New York, N.Y. 10010

Cover art by Doug Beekman
Illustrations by Todd Cameron Hamilton

ISBN: 0-812-56406-5
CAN. ED.: 0-812-56407-3

Printed in the United States of America

0 9 8 7 6 5 4 3 2 1

# C. J. CHERRYH'S
# MORGAINE

ONCE UPON A TIME and far away, the species who called themselves the *qhal* went to space and, on a barren world of their own solar system, discovered a matter-transport gate of unknown origins.

They built another and discovered it was possible to send an object (or living being) not only between there and the other world, but also to a later *time* on that world, by aiming it at where that world would *be*, in the course of its orbit about their sun. And vice versa.

If it worked here, they reasoned, why not further?

So they built other gates, using spaceships only to carry the technology to the worlds they meant to colonize. They developed starflight, but used it only because they wanted more room, more worlds, more gates—and they discovered a great lure within the gates: the bored, the restless, those with personal reasons to leave not only their homes but present time, migrated

1

through the gates to the future in greater and greater numbers.

It was forbidden, absolutely forbidden, to go into the past, for fear someone might alter something minor, and thereby alter all history to follow. Therefore there was no way to return home, once through the gates on a time-jump.

And the future never satisfied. For someone willing to jump once, further jumps promised . . . perhaps the better life, the luck, the happiness that was always out of reach.

Some amused themselves by stealing beasts and qhal-like species from other worlds, creating civilizations, watching them develop by skipping from century to century, interfering here and there and skipping ahead to see the result. They became like gods.

But their most distant future grew strange, overcrowded with such time-travelers: the world grew over-populated . . . miserable and rife with crime and dissolution, among people, who, seeing age after age in this condition, refused to go further. More, people's *memories* began to fail them. History seemed to shift daily, what was known truth might change tomorrow and people began to whisper that those who went out the gates beyond this point in time . . . went to their deaths, for the gates failed here, and ended.

Perhaps someone had fled into the past and done the unthinkable: changed history.

Perhaps all local space-time was warped beyond its ability to remain stable.

For whatever reason, there was a time-implosion: space-time repaired itself, flung all the elements into one universal Now, one single moment from which all time began again, on all the worlds within this area of space.

It was long after that, that the human species went starfaring, and found the region, and a barren world, and the Gate.

Human archaeologists unraveled the story from buried records. They realized to their horror that one of the species the qhal had raided was humankind, somewhere in Earth's Dark Ages.

They chose a hundred men and women to go through that gate and close it, a hundred who knew there was no possible return.

But that gate led them to another gate, and another and another: their fears were true.

And although the members of the team were killed, one by one, by accident and war in the gate-worlds, they birthed heirs to their mission, some totally human, some not—for the qhal had tampered with genetics, among other things.

At the last, only five survived, and one, using qhalur knowledge, forged a sword of gate-stuff, powered by the gates, a sword that is a gate itself—a doomsday weapon.

But it did not save four of them. And the last survivor was a woman with the look of a qhal: Morgaine is her name; she carries the sword;

and she survives held in stasis within a gate until a young warrior frees her by accident.

His name is Nhi Vanye i Chya. He is an outlaw. He is altogether human—bastard son of the lord of clan Nhi, in Morija.

His father Nhi Rijan begot him in revenge, on a lady of clan Chya, a prisoner in a minor war of the sort common since Morgaine the witch took the Kingdom down in chaos, since there was no longer a High King to hold the clans together. But Vanye turned out a precocious and affectionate child, and won his father's grudging acceptance, after his mother's early death. Seeing how readily Vanye took to arms and horses (and attributing it to his bloodline in the boy) he took Vanye in among his legitimate sons, Kandrys and Erij, intending to have Vanye grow up in the house, achieve warrior's rank, and become a respected captain in the service of his heir Kandrys.

The fact was that Vanye was very good; and half-Chya; and Kandrys hated him from their boyhood . . . constantly teased and tormented him, lured Erij into the nasty game, and the game went on for years, increasingly dangerous, increasingly cruel.

Vanye never complained, being a boy who had no mother to go to for advice, and a father who, he thought, would be angry at any weakness in him, and who would naturally take Kandrys' and Erij's side. So he kept silent about what his brothers did. He played the game, as he thought, fairly, as cleverly as he could, and being youngest, generally lost.

Mostly he hoped Kandrys and Erij would learn to respect him. And that his father would come to love him, not merely tolerate him. He worked at weapons-practice, he learned horses, he learned every scrap Kandrys' teachers would throw his way in an idle moment.

And at eighteen he won the man's braid, the rank of a Nhi warrior, after which no one could affront him without expecting legitimate challenge.

But his brothers were outraged at this honor Rijan gave him.

And under the guise of a practice-bout to try the new warrior, Nhi Kandrys who had had *his* braid for more than two years, attacked him in earnest.

Vanye realized it and reacted instinctively, when Kandrys made a move that was in earnest —and he was very, very good. Erij saw it coming and moved to stop it—but too late. Kandrys lost his life, Erij lost most of his right hand, and Nhi Rijan demanded Vanye's suicide to atone for the crime.

He was hardly eighteen. He did not want to die. His father called him coward, cut off his warrior's braid to brand him a felon and a coward, and, because he would not hang one of his own sons, condemned Vanye to be *ilin*, a wandering fighter little better than an outlaw, and able to be Claimed by any lord from whom he accepts food and fire-warmth. Within their religion, an *ilin* must serve that lord, when Claimed, for one year, unless the lord should free him sooner—obeying any order he is given: the lord acquires any guilt for what actions he orders—the *ilin* is free of that—but *ilin* can be badly treated, sent into impossible situations, even killed by his lord without cause or reason.

If he breaks that oath, he is damned to hell, and only his lord's forgiveness can save him.

Still, if he dies obeying orders, or lives to the end of his year, he has saved his soul, and if he lives, can again call himself a free warrior—and settle accounts in his own right.

Vanye avoided Claiming by his dead brother's relatives, which would have been terrible enough.

He did not remember until, half-starved on a winter night, he accepted a bit of venison at Morgaine's fireside,—that there was one woman who had been given the status of lord among the Chya, a hundred years before his birth.

And to serve a qhal—is sufficient unto itself to damn a man's soul, as surely as oath-breaking or murder.

# INTRODUCTION AND RULES TO CROSSROADS™ ADVENTURES
## by Bill Fawcett

FOR THE MANY of us who have enjoyed the stories upon which this adventure is based, it may seem a bit strange to find an introduction this long at the start of a book. What you are holding is both a game and an adventure. Have you ever read a book and then told yourself you would have been able to think more clearly or seen a way out of the hero's dilemma? In a Crossroads™ adventure you have the opportunity to do just that. *You* make the key decisions. By means of a few easily followed steps you are able to see the results of your choices.

A Crossroads™ adventure is as much fun to read as it is to play. It is more than just a game or a book. It is a chance to enjoy once more a familiar and treasured story. The excitement of adventuring in a beloved universe is neatly blended into a story which stands well on its own merit, a story in which you will encounter many familiar characters and places and discover more than a few new ones as well. Each adventure is a thrilling tale, with the extra suspense and satisfaction of knowing that you will succeed or fail by your own endeavors.

# THE ADVENTURE

Throughout the story you will have the opportunity to make decisions. Each of these decisions will affect whether the hero succeeds in the quest, or even survives. In some cases you will actually be fighting battles; other times you will use your knowledge and instincts to choose the best path to follow. In many cases there will be clues in the story or illustrations.

A Crossroads™ adventure is divided into sections. The length of a section may be a few lines or many pages. The section numbers are shown at the top of a page to make it easier for you to follow. Each section ends when you must make a decision, or fight. The next section you turn to will show the results of your decision. At least one six-sided die and a pencil are needed to "play" this book.

The words "six-sided dice" are often abbreviated as "D6." If more than one is needed a number will precede the term. "Roll three

six-sided dice" will be written as "Roll 3 D6."
Virtually all the die rolls in these rules do
involve rolling three six-sided dice (or rolling
one six-sided die three times) and totaling what
is rolled.

If you are an experienced role play gamer,
you may also wish to convert the values given in
this novel to those you can use with any fantasy
role-playing game you are now playing with. All
of the adventures have been constructed so that
they also can be easily adapted in this manner.
The values for the hero may transfer directly.
While fantasy games are much more compli-
cated, doing this will allow you to be the Game
Master for other players. Important values for
the hero's opponents will be given to aid you in
this conversion and to give those playing by the
Crossroads™ rules a better idea of what they are
facing.

## THE HERO

Seven values are used to describe the hero in
gaming terms. These are strength, intelligence,
wisdom/luck, constitution, dexterity, charisma,
and hit points. These values measure all of a
character's abilities. At the end of these rules is
a Record Sheet. On it are given all of the values
for the hero of this adventure and any equipment or supplies he begins the adventure with.

While you adventure, this record can be used to keep track of damage received and any new equipment or magical items acquired. You may find it advisable to make a photocopy of that page. Permission to do so, for your own use only, is given by the publisher of this game/novel. You may wish to consult this record sheet as we discuss what each of the values represents.

# STRENGTH

This is the measure of how physically powerful your hero is. It compares the hero to others in how much the character can lift, how hard he can punch, and just how brawny he is. The strongest a normal human can be is to have a strength value of 18. The weakest a child would have is a 3. Here is a table giving comparable strengths:

| Strength | Example |
|---|---|
| 3 | A five year old child |
| 6 | An elderly man |
| 8 | Out of shape and over 40 |
| 10 | An average 20 year old man |
| 13 | In good shape and works out |
| 15 | A top athlete or football running back |
| 17 | Changes auto tires without a jack |

| 18 | Arm wrestles Arnold Schwarzenegger and wins |

A Tolkien-style troll, being magical, might have a strength of 19 or 20. A full-grown elephant has a strength of 23. A fifty-foot dragon would have a strength of 30.

# INTELLIGENCE

Being intelligent is not just a measure of native brain power. It is also an indication of the ability to use that intelligence. The value for intelligence also measures how aware the character is, and so how likely they are to notice a subtle clue. Intelligence can be used to measure how resistant a mind is to hypnosis or mental attack. A really sharp baboon would have an intelligence of 3. Most humans (we all know exceptions) begin at about 5. The highest value possible is an 18. Here is a table of relative intelligence:

| Intelligence | Example |
|---|---|
| 3 | My dog |
| 5 | Lassie |
| 6 | Curly (the third Stooge) |
| 8 | Somewhat slow |
| 10 | Average person |

Brainiac of comicbook fame would have a value of 21.

## WISDOM/LUCK

Wisdom is the ability to make correct judgments, often with less than complete facts. Wisdom is knowing what to do and when to do it. Attacking, when running will earn you a spear in the back, is the best part of wisdom. Being in the right place at the right time can be called luck or wisdom. Not being discovered when hiding can be luck, if it is because you knew enough to not hide in the poison oak, wisdom is also a factor. Activities which are based more on instinct, the intuitive leap, than analysis are decided by wisdom.

In many ways both wisdom and luck are further connected, especially as wisdom also measures how friendly the ruling powers of the universe (not the author, the fates) are to the hero. A hero may be favored by fate or luck because he is reverent or for no discernible reason at all. This will give them a high wisdom value. Everyone knows those "lucky" individuals who can fall in the mud and find a gold coin. Here is a table measuring relative wisdom/luck:

| Wisdom | Example |
| --- | --- |
| Under 3 | Cursed or totally unthinking |
| 5 | Never plans, just reacts |
| 7 | Some cunning, "street smarts" |
| 9 | Average thinking person |
| 11 | Skillful planner, good gambler |
| 13 | Successful businessman/Lee Iacocca |
| 15 | Captain Kirk (wisdom)/Conan (luck) |
| 17 | Sherlock Holmes (wisdom)/Luke Skywalker (luck) |
| 18 | Lazarus Long |

# CONSTITUTION

The more you can endure, the higher your constitution. If you have a high constitution you are better able to survive physical damage, emotional stress, and poisons. The higher your value for constitution, the longer you are able to continue functioning in a difficult situation. A character with a high constitution can run farther (though not necessarily faster) or hang by one hand longer than the average person. A high constitution means you also have more stamina, and recover more quickly from injuries. A comparison of values for constitution:

| Constitution | Example |
| --- | --- |
| 3 | A terminal invalid |
| 6 | A ten year old child |
| 8 | Your stereotyped "98 pound weakling" |
| 10 | Average person |
| 14 | Olympic athlete/Sam Spade |
| 16 | Marathon runner/Rocky |
| 18 | Rasputin/Batman |

A whale would have a constitution of 20. Superman's must be about 50.

## DEXTERITY

The value for dexterity measures not only how fast a character can move, but how well-coordinated those movements are. A surgeon, a pianist, and a juggler all need a high value for dexterity. If you have a high value for dexterity you can react quickly (though not necessarily correctly), duck well, and perform sleight of hand magic (if you are bright enough to learn how). Conversely, a low dexterity means you react slowly and drop things frequently. All other things being equal, the character with the highest dexterity will have the advantage of the first attack in a combat. Here are some comparative examples of dexterity:

| Dexterity | Example |
|-----------|---------|
| 3 or less | Complete klutz |
| 5 | Inspector Clouseau |
| 6 | Can walk and chew gum, most of the time |
| 8 | Barney Fife |
| 10 | Average person |
| 13 | Good fencer/Walter Payton |
| 15 | Brain surgeon/Houdini |
| 16 | Flying Karamazov Brothers |
| 17 | Movie ninja/Cyrano de Bergerac |
| 18 | Bruce Lee |

Batman, Robin, Daredevil and The Shadow all have a dexterity of 19. At a dexterity of 20 you don't even see the man move before he has taken your wallet and underwear and has left the room (the Waco Kid).

# CHARISMA

Charisma is more than just good looks, though they certainly don't hurt. It is a measure of how persuasive a hero is and how willing others are to do what he wants. You can have average looks yet be very persuasive, and have a high charisma. If your value for charisma is high, you are better able to talk yourself out of trouble or obtain information from a stranger. If your charisma is low, you may be ignored or even mocked, even when you are right. A high charisma value is vital to entertainers of any sort, and leaders. A different type of charisma is just as important to spies. In the final measure a high value for charisma means people will react to you in the way you desire. Here are some comparative values for charisma:

| Charisma | Example |
| --- | --- |
| 3 | Hunchback of Notre Dame |
| 5 | An ugly used car salesman |
| 7 | Richard Nixon today |
| 10 | Average person |
| 12 | Team coach |
| 14 | Magnum, P.I. |
| 16 | Henry Kissinger/Jim DiGriz |
| 18 | Dr.Who/Prof. Harold Hill (Centauri) |

# HIT POINTS

Hit points represent the total amount of damage a hero can take before he is killed or knocked out. You can receive damage from being wounded in a battle, through starvation, or even through a mental attack. Hit points measure more than just how many times the hero can be battered over the head before he is knocked out. They also represent the ability to keep striving toward a goal. A poorly paid mercenary may have only a few hit points, even though he is a hulking brute of a man, because the first time he receives even a slight wound he will withdraw from the fight. A blacksmith's apprentice who won't accept defeat will have a higher number of hit points.

A character's hit points can be lost through a wound to a specific part of the body or through general damage to the body itself. This general damage can be caused by a poison, a bad fall, or even exhaustion and starvation. Pushing your body too far beyond its limits may result in a successful action at the price of the loss of a few hit points. All these losses are treated in the same manner.

Hit points lost are subtracted from the total on the hero's record sheet. When a hero has lost all of his hit points, then that character has failed. When this happens you will be told to which section to turn. Here you will often find a description of the failure and its consequences for the hero.

The hit points for the opponents the hero meets in combat are given in the adventure. You should keep track of these hit points on a piece of scrap paper. When a monster or opponent has lost all of its hit points, it has lost the fight. If a character is fighting more than one opponent, then you should keep track of each of their hit points. Each will continue to fight until it has 0 hit points. When everyone on one side of the battle has no hit points left, the combat is over.

Even the best played character can lose all of his hit points when you roll too many bad dice during a combat. If the hero loses all of his hit points, the adventure may have ended in failure. You will be told so in the next section you are instructed to turn to. In this case you can turn back to the first section and begin again. This time you will have the advantage of having learned some of the hazards the hero will face.

## TAKING CHANCES

There will be occasions where you will have to decide whether the hero should attempt to perform some action which involves risk. This might be to climb a steep cliff, jump a pit, or juggle three daggers. There will be other cases where it might benefit the hero to notice something subtle or remember an ancient ballad perfectly. In all of these cases you will be asked to roll three six-sided dice (3 D6) and compare the total of all three dice to the hero's value for the appropriate ability.

For example, if the hero is attempting to juggle three balls, then for him to do so successfully you would have to roll a total equal to or less than the hero's value for dexterity. If your total was less than this dexterity value, then you would be directed to a section describing how the balls looked as they were skillfully juggled. If you rolled a higher value than that for dexterity, then you would be told to read a section which describes the embarrassment of dropping the balls, and being laughed at by the audience.

Where the decision is a judgment call, such as whether to take the left or right staircase, it is left entirely to you. It will be likely that somewhere in the adventure or in the original novels there will be some piece of information which would indicate that the left staircase leads to a trap and the right to your goal. No die roll will be needed for a judgment decision.

In all cases you will be guided at the end of each section as to exactly what you need do. If you have any questions you should refer back to these rules.


# MAGICAL ITEMS AND SPECIAL EQUIPMENT

There are many unusual items which appear in the pages of this adventure. When it is possible for them to be taken by the hero, you will be given the option of doing so. One or more of these items may be necessary to the successful completion of the adventure. You will be given the option of taking these at the end of a section.

If you choose to pick up an item and succeed in getting it, you should list that item on the hero's record sheet. There is no guarantee that deciding to take an item means you will actually obtain it. If someone owns it already they are quite likely to resent your efforts to take it. In some cases things may not even be all they appear to be or the item may be trapped or cursed. Having it may prove a detriment rather than a benefit.

All magical items give the hero a bonus (or penalty) on certain die rolls. You will be told when this applies, and often given the option of whether or not to use the item. You will be instructed at the end of the section on how many points to add to or subtract from your die roll. If you choose to use an item which can function only once, such as a magic potion or hand grenade, then you will also be instructed to remove the item from your record sheet. Certain items, such as a magic sword, can be used many times. In this case you will be told when you obtain the item when you can apply the bonus. The bonus for a magic sword could be added every time a character is in hand to hand combat.

Other special items may allow a character to fly, walk through fire, summon magical warriors, or many other things. How and when they affect play will again be told to you in the paragraphs at the end of the sections where you have the choice of using them.

Those things which restore lost hit points are a special case. You may choose to use these at any time during the adventure. If you have a magical healing potion which returns 1 D6 of lost hit points, you may add these points when you think it is best to. This can even be during a combat in the place of a round of attack. No matter how many healing items you use, a character can never have more hit points than he began the adventure with.

There is a limit to the number of special items any character may carry. In any Crossroads™ adventure the limit is four items. If you already have four special items listed on your record sheet, then one of these must be discarded in order to take the new item. Any time you erase an item off the record sheet, whether because it was used or because you wish to add a new item, whatever is erased is permanently lost. It can never be "found" again, even if you return to the same location later in the adventure.

Except for items which restore hit points, the hero can only use an item in combat or when given the option to do so. The opportunity will be listed in the instructions.

In the case of an item which can be used in every combat, the bonus can be added or subtracted as the description of the item indicates. A +2 sword would add two points to any total rolled in combat. This bonus would be used each and every time the hero attacks. Only one attack bonus can be used at a time. Just because a hero has both a +1 and a +2 sword doesn't mean he knows how to fight with both at once. Only the better bonus would apply.

If a total of 12 is needed to hit an attacking monster and the hero has a +2 sword, then you will only need to roll a total of 10 on the three dice to successfully strike the creature.

You could also find an item, perhaps enchanted armor, which could be worn in all combat and would have the effect of subtracting its bonus from the total of any opponents' attack on its wearer. (Bad guys can wear magic armor, too.) If a monster normally would need a 13 to hit a character who has obtained a set of +2 armor, then the monster would now need a total of 15 to score a hit. An enchanted shield would operate in the same way, but could never be used when the character was using a weapon which needed both hands, such as a pike, long-bow or two-handed sword.

# COMBAT

There will be many situations where the hero will be forced, or you may choose, to meet an opponent in combat. The opponents can vary from a wild beast, to a human thief, or an unearthly monster. In all cases the same steps are followed.

The hero will attack first in most combats unless you are told otherwise. This may happen when there is an ambush, other special situations, or because the opponent simply has a much higher dexterity.

At the beginning of a combat section you will be given the name or type of opponent involved. For each combat five values are given. The first of these is the total on three six-sided dice needed for the attacker to hit the hero. Next to this value is the value the hero needs to hit these opponents. After these two values are listed the hit points of the opponent. If there is more than one opponent, each one will have the same number. (See the Hit Points section included earlier if you are unclear as to what these do.) Under the value needed to hit by the opponent is the hit points of damage that it will do to the hero when it attacks successfully. Finally, under the total needed for the hero to successfully hit an opponent is the damage he will do with the different weapons he might have. Unlike a check for completing a daring action (where you wish to roll under a value), in a combat you have to roll the value given or higher on three six-sided dice to successfully hit an opponent.

For example:

Here is how a combat between the hero armed with a sword and three brigands armed only with daggers is written:

*BRIGANDS*
*To hit the hero: 14    To be hit: 12    Hit points: 4*

*Damage with daggers:*   *Damage with sword:*
*1 D6 (used by the*   *2 D6 (used by the hero)*
*brigands)*

*There are three brigands. If two are killed (taken to 0 hit points) the third will flee in panic.*

*If the hero wins, turn to section 85.*

*If he is defeated, turn to section 67.*


## RUNNING AWAY

Running rather than fighting, while often desirable, is not always possible. The option to run away is available only when listed in the choices. Even when this option is given, there is no guarantee the hero can get away safely.


## THE COMBAT SEQUENCE

Any combat is divided into alternating rounds. In most cases the hero will attack first. Next, surviving opponents will have the chance to fight back. When both have attacked, one round will have been completed. A combat can have any number of rounds and continues until the hero or his opponents are defeated. Each round is the equivalent of six seconds. During this time all the parties in the combat may actually take more than one swing at each other.

The steps in resolving a combat in which the hero attacks first are as follows:

1.  Roll three six-sided dice. Total the numbers showing on all three and add any bonuses from weapons or special circumstances. If this total is the same or greater than the second value given, "to hit the opponent," then the hero has successfully attacked.

2.  If the hero attacks successfully, the next step is to determine how many hit points of damage he did to the opponent. The die roll for this will be given below the "to hit opponent" information.

3.  Subtract any hit points of damage done from the opponent's total.

4.  If any of the enemy have one or more hit points left, then the remaining opponent or opponents now can attack. Roll three six-sided dice for each attacker. Add up each of these sets of three dice. If the total is the same or greater than the value listed after "to hit the hero" in the section describing the combat, the attack was successful.

5.  For each hit, roll the number of dice listed for damage. Subtract the total from the

number of hit points the hero has at that time. Enter the new, lower total on the hero's record sheet.

If both the hero and one or more opponents have hit points left, the combat continues. Start again at step one. The battle ends only when the hero is killed, all the opponents are killed or all of one side has run away. A hero cannot, except through a healing potion or spells or when specifically told to during the adventure, regain lost hit points. A number of small wounds from several opponents will kill a character as thoroughly as one titanic, unsuccessful combat with a hill giant.

## DAMAGE

The combat continues, following the sequence given below, until either the hero or his opponents have no hit points. In the case of multiple opponents, subtract hit points from one opponent until the total reaches 0 or less. Extra hit points of damage done on the round when each opponent is defeated are lost. They do not carry over to the next enemy in·the group. To win the combat, you must eliminate all of an opponent's hit points.

The damage done by a weapon will vary depending on who is using it. A club in the hands of a child will do far less damage than the same club wielded by a hill giant. The maximum damage is given as a number of six-sided dice. In some cases the maximum will be less than a whole die. This is abbreviated by a minus sign followed by a number. For example D6–2, meaning one roll of a six-sided die, minus two. The total damage can never be less than zero, meaning no damage done. 2 D6–1 means that you should roll two six-sided dice and then subtract one from the total of them both.

A combat may, because of the opponent involved, have one or more special circumstances. It may be that the enemy will surrender or flee when its hit point total falls below a certain level, or even that reinforcements will arrive to help the bad guys after so many rounds. You will be told of these special situations in the lines directly under the combat values.

Now you may turn to section one.

# RECORD SHEET
## Nhi Vanye i Chya

Strength: 14

Intelligence: 12

Wisdom: 08

Constitution: 13

Dexterity: 15

Charisma: 07

Hit Points: 24

Magic Items
1.
2.
3.
4.

Equipment and weapons carried:
1. Armor
2. Longsword
3. Dagger

# * 1 *

The fire embers glow dully, giving up their last fading light. Vanye wearily forces his eyes open and stares at the remains of the fire. He is crouching on the ground before the crackling husks of burning logs. His eyes steal carefully around the perimeter of the camp. It looks secure. His eyes rest on Morgaine's sleeping form. She is huddled beneath a worn blanket, her breathing shallow. Her wound is severe, and its slow healing robs her of all her vigor.

Vanye shivers to look at her. Morgaine, the inhuman witch of ancient legends. The woman who had led ten thousand men to their deaths one hundred years ago. And now here she was again: alive and on a mad quest for vengeance. Vanye studies her, drawn to her as a sparrow is to a cobra. She is tall, tanned, and bears a striking mane of white hair, just as the legends said. She is almost beautiful, with a quiet regal beauty. . . . With a surge of self-control, Vanye stops his mind from wandering further, and shakes his head violently, as if to clear it of a dreadful thought.

He slowly stirs the fire. The glowing embers leap into fresh flame. He gently places a handful of dried leaves on the embers. As the leaves begin smoldering, he adds fresh wood. Flames, untamed and elemental, crackle along the dried sticks, sending a rush of heat over his face.

Turning slowly away from Morgaine, Vanye rocks back on his haunches and listens to the stillness of the night.

Weariness creeps over him and he forces his eyes open again. During his life as a warrior in his father's keep, Vanye spent many nights standing guard before watchfires. He is familiar with the grueling routines and hardships a warrior is expected to endure. But since becoming *ilin*, and a warrior-servant to Morgaine, it seems he is spending all his time either riding or sitting up before watchfires. His bleary eyes cannot quite recall their last full night of blissful sleep. He can barely remember a time when his muscles did not ache and feel stiff. But despite the dull, constant pain of his many wounds, Vanye feels a strange elation, as if he is alive for the first time in his life. Alive, and curiously powerful.

Morgaine.

He lets his eyes droop shut again. Images play upon his eyelids. He sees Morij-keep, his ancestral home Ra-morij, where his father rules. He scowls as visions of his two half-brothers' cruelty floats across his mind's eye. He remembers their cruel jests, their insults, and the times that pranks had gotten out of hand and almost killed him. But worst of all was the contempt that laced their every word—the cold scorn in every smile. All because Vanye is a bastard. Because his mother was a kidnapped woman of Chya.

But bastard or not, he is son of Nhi Rijan. He is of noble blood, and trained as his brothers' equal. Through perseverance and might he earned the right to wear the warrior's braids. And his brothers could not abide that. Nhi Erij had grudgingly accepted Vanye's accomplishment, but the elder, Nhi Kandrys, felt Vanye's warrior status was an insult to the family blood, and his hatred of Vanye increased.

As the three brothers grew, pranks of children became the malice of men. Malice that one day erupted in blood.

Vanye sees the blood before his eyes: his brother's blood. He sees the longsword in his hand rise and fall, rise and fall on the body of his brother Kandrys. He sees his armorless brother Erij intervene to try to stop the blow, and come away with his right hand butchered for his trouble. It doesn't matter that Kandrys attacked Vanye during a practice bout, or that Vanye had not meant to kill. All that matters is that Kandrys was the beloved of their father the Nhi Lord Rijan, and the lord raged that Kandrys is dead and Vanye alive.

Still in his half-sleep, Vanye's throat burns as he relives his greatest shame. He was unable to kill himself when his father demanded it. He had chosen loss of honor over loss of life. Perhaps it was his Chya heritage. His mother's people were known to have an unquenchable thirst for life that often exceeded the narrow bounds of Nhi honor.

Nevertheless, for refusing to slit open his belly with his Honor Sword, Nhi Rijan made Vanye an honorless, outcast *ilin*, forced to wander until Claimed for a year's service by any lord who wished. *Ilinin* seldom survived their year's service, but honorable death in the service of a worthy master is considered expiation for an *ilin's* crimes, and his soul can reclaim its honor in death.

For two years Vanye had eluded a Claiming. Then he had met Morgaine.

Vanye awoke with a start, raising his head quickly and sitting upright. The visions from the past flee like morning mist. He strains to listen.

The noise comes again. A faint rustling. Something is moving just beyond the perimeter of the camp; moving cautiously and quietly. Vanye peers into the blackness, but the noise comes from beyond the light of the fire. Gently and silently, he eases his longsword from its sheath.

*If Vanye should charge into the brush and attack whatever is moving, turn to section 2.*

*If Vanye should enter the brush cautiously to investigate, turn to section 3.*

*If Vanye should remain seated and continue to observe, turn to section 4.*

# * 2 *

Vanye hears the noise again. There is definitely something out there, just beyond the light of the watchfire. If it were a friend, it would surely have identified itself by now. Vanye scowls at the thought of being taken by surprise. Without warning he leaps to his feet, and charges into the undergrowth.

At reflex speed Vanye sees a motion on the ground, and swings at it with his longsword. He hears a pitiful squeal, and feels his sword lay flesh open. He looks down, and sees a dead rabbit.

Vanye sighs, the battle fever broken. He feels more than a little foolish. Tension fades from his muscles. He picks up the still warm rabbit and inspects it. At least they have fresh meat for the next day.

*Turn to section 5.*

## * **3** *

Vanye listens carefully. The night is very quiet. Then, out of the stillness, he hears the noise again. It is a quiet rustling. It is keeping its distance from him, but edging its way around the camp on quiet feet. A friend would have identified himself by now. Vanye quietly gets to his feet. He slips quickly and quietly into the undergrowth just beyond the range of the firelight. If he is being observed, at least the spy can no longer see him. The rustling noise increases, and becomes frantic.

He moves quietly, smoothly through the underbrush. His hunter's training comes back to him easily; instinctively. Vanye has no trouble pinpointing the source of the sound and closing on it. He looks down, and sees a fat, frightened rabbit plunging through the coarse brush.

Vanye approaches the little creature silently, and when he is beside it, bends down and looks it in the eye. The rabbit freezes, paralyzed for an instant, with terror. Vanye says, "Shoo!" and the rabbit bounds off in terror, scurrying for the protection of the deep forest.

*Turn to section 5.*

* **4** *

Vanye sits calmly before the fire, holding his sword tightly, but in a way that looks unconcerned and casual. He continues listening to the quiet noises of the night.

The rustling sound continues to wind its way along the edge of the camp. Vanye turns his body slowly, following the sound.

The undergrowth rustles again, and a large rabbit suddenly hops out of the bushes. It stares at Vanye for a moment, then turns its bushy tail and flees into the brush.

Vanye relaxes his tense grip on his sword and eases it back into its sheath with a smile. The little creature can live another day. He leans forward to stir the fire back to life.

*Turn to section 5.*

## * **5** *

Vanye returns to his mat and crouches down to continue his watch. The night is still young. It will be a long watch.

He props himself up on his sword and rocks gently back and forth to keep awake. The fire crackles quietly, and peacefully. Warmth washes over him, and Vanye is slowly lulled into a complacent languor.

But his half-sleep is not restful. Again images spill across his eyes, visions of desperate travel in the frozen mountains, pursued by the Myya of Morij-Erd. For two long years he lived as an outcast, evading patrols and shunning all company, in an attempt to reach Aenor-Pyvvn, and the safety of friends. Those were unhappy times, and he clamps his eyes more tightly shut to dispel the thoughts they bring to mind.

Blissful stillness returns to his mind, but does not last long. New images are soon racing past his mind's eye. He sees his horse galloping frantically across an accursed valley of ancient standing stones. The wounded buck he was chasing could not last long with an arrow in its flanks.

The deer ran toward the double monolith

known as Morgaine's Tomb, as if its pain told it that it had less to fear from ancient, evil magics than from Vanye's gray-fletched arrows. Vanye began to grow afraid, but his hunger was stronger than his fear. But then he saw the Witchfire.

The very air between the twin pillars of Morgaine's Tomb glowed and shimmered with an eerie light that caused the landscape seen through the pillars to ripple and distort. The buck plunged into the shimmering field, and was gone. Vanye grew cold. As he watched, a form appeared in the shimmering light of the Witchfires.

A woman's form.

Morgaine.

He felt terror and awe all at once. He wanted to run and he wanted to stay. In the end, he stayed, and because of that decision, and others made (or mismade) soon afterwards, he was bound to serve Morgaine. Though such service may damn his soul, he is bound to serve her faithfully. For his soul is surely damned if he at the thought of this dilemma breaks his oath and refuses a rightful Claiming.

At the thought of this dilemma Vanye twitches in his sleep and almost wakes.

Then he fades back to sleep and recalls more of that fateful night.

Morgaine emerged from the bright hypnotic glow that spilled from between the pillars. She descended the hill, coming toward him, astride Siptah, her gray stallion, her mane of white hair and her white fur cloak drifting like an illusion against the snow of the hill. He watched, transfixed, as she rode up to him. He knew who she was. But she was supposed to be dead, one hundred years dead. How could she be riding up to him now?

The visions in Vanye's sleep-muddled head raced forward. He watched again as Morgaine, young and seemingly still very much alive, shared her food and shelter with him and exercised her right as a lord to Claim Vanye for a year's service. He was *ilin* and acknowledged her right. In performing the Claiming, Morgaine bound Vanye to serve her faithfully even unto death. For the next year he must serve a despised, long-dead witch who was hated for her part in wars long past. Ten thousand who had followed her had perished at the hands of the immortal sorcerer Thiye. Was he fated to join them?

Her only obligation to him is to look after his needs. He has no choice but to follow her. It is the only way he can recover his honor. Abandoning her or disobeying her would damn his soul forever.

So she led them to the ravaged plains of Koris. Her goal was to destroy the Witchfire at Hjemur, and in so doing destroy all the evil magic it had allowed to pass into the world. *This* world, which she told him was but one of many. She would ride into the heart of evil, and as her *ilin*, wherever she rode he must follow. If she fails in her quest, Vanye was oath-bound to complete it. So if *she* failed, he was bound to fight the sorcerer Thiye, the author of all evil in the world, and reputed to be more ancient even than Morgaine.

Vanye came awake suddenly; another noise . . . as distinct as the first, but more cautious.

*If Vanye should charge into the brush and attack whatever is moving, turn to section 6.*

*If Vanye should enter the brush cautiously to investigate, turn to section 7.*

*If Vanye should remain seated and continue to observe, turn to section 8.*

# * **6** *

Vanye's mind is no longer fogged with sleep and burning memory. He is cool and sharp. He leaps to his feet, drawing his longsword in one smooth move. He hurtles into the dark underbrush, alert for any motion. A streak of black fur leaps toward him, snarling. He strikes at it with his sword, and only after his swing does he realize what it is. It is a Koris Wolf; a savage, unnatural beast created by fell magics, killers not hunters. It is one of the many beasts created by Thiye of Hjemur, the same man he was bound to kill.

KORIS WOLF
*To hit Vanye: 13   To be hit: 9   Hit Points: 8*
*Damage with claws   Damage with*
*and fangs: 1 D6+1   longsword: 2 D6*
*                    Damage with dagger: 1 D6*

*The Koris Wolf attacks with a ruthless savagery. It will fight until it kills or is killed.*

*If Vanye kills the Koris Wolf, turn to section 17.*

*If the wolf kills Vanye, turn to section 29.*

*If Vanye should turn and run away into the woods, roll an extra attack on Vanye, and turn to section 13.*

## * **7** *

Vanye listens intently to the woods. The noises of the night are quieter than ever before. He quietly picks up his longsword, stands, and pads softly away into the underbrush. Once he is beyond the dim light of the dying fire, he stops and listens. He hears the sound again, a soft padding. He circles around the noise, moving deeper into the woods. Then he sees it, a Koris Wolf.

Normal wolves are predators. They hunt and kill small creatures, but generally avoid men except during the cruelest winters. Koris Wolves are different. They are one of the mad sorcerer Thiye's gifts to the ravaged plains of Koris. They kill for pleasure rather than food, and seem to take a special delight in attacking men.

The huge wolf still has its back to him. It is studying Morgaine with a predator's eye.

*If Vanye should attack the Koris Wolf from behind, roll 3 dice. If the roll is less than Vanye's Dexterity, he has taken the Koris Wolf by surprise. Turn to section 11.*

© 1986

## Section 7

*If he attacks and the roll is more than Vanye's Dexterity, turn to section 15.*

*If Vanye should return to camp, turn to section 18.*

*If Vanye should turn and run away into the woods, turn to section 13.*

## *  **8**  *

Vanye listens to the night noises. He hears the light footfall again. Another rabbit, he muses. He is tired of chasing rabbits. And if it is trouble, he would do better to allow it to come to him than to go after it.

His musings are interrupted by an unexpected silence. He did not hear the noise retreat. It is just suddenly no longer there. Vanye begins to grow uneasy.

He hears a snarl behind him and whirls around. He isn't fast enough. Sharp claws rake along his mail shirt and bite into the flesh of his back. He winces in pain as the attacking creature lands on the ground before him. It is a Koris Wolf, an unnatural beast bred by the sorceries of Thiye of Hjemur, created to be a killer of men; the lancets of pain in his back attest to that.

*Vanye just took 4 points of damage. Mark them off before continuing the fight. Vanye will attack first in the combat round as usual, now that the Koris Wolf has made its surprise attack.*

KORIS WOLF
*To hit Vanye: 12    To be hit: 10    Hit Points: 8*

## Section 8

*Koris Wolf*

*Damage with claws and fangs: 1 D6+1*

*Damage with longsword: 2 D6*
*Damage with dagger: 1 D6*

*The Koris Wolf attacks with a ruthless savagery. It will fight until it kills or is killed.*

*If Vanye kills the Koris Wolf, turn to section 17.*

*If the Koris Wolf kills Vanye, turn to section 29.*

*If Vanye should turn and run into the woods before combat begins, roll a free attack on Vanye for the Koris Wolf, and turn to section 13.*

*If Vanye should turn and run away into the woods at anytime during the fight, roll an extra attack for the Wolf, and turn to section 13.*

# * 9 *

Morgaine peers at Vanye in the half-light. "Are thee hurt?"

"It is nothing," Vanye replies, and continues to repair his damaged armor.

Morgaine opens her travelling bag. "Thee may be mended easily," she said.

He looks with fear at the strange *qujalin* tools that spilled from her kit. There are small metal canisters and delicate, intricate utensils. Vanye trembles to look at them. They are as foul and ancient in his eyes as all the evil in the world. And yet Vanye had seen Morgaine's wounds heal rapidly under the influence of their sorcerous compounds. But Morgaine was undoubtedly *qujal* . . . it was only right that *qujalin* medicine would help her . . . and yet . . .

Vanye's mind is wracked with doubts.

*If Vanye should accept the sorcerous medicine, turn to section 14.*

*If Vanye should reject the offer of assistance, turn to section 25.*

# ∗ **10** ∗

With Morgaine's voice still ringing through the woods, Vanye heads away from the campsite. By morning he will be beyond all concern.

As he walks, Vanye tastes the bitter ashes of humiliation. He feels a great sorrow well up in him, worse somehow, than when he was cast out of his home in Ra-morij. His leaving now is of his own choice. So why, he wonders, does it hurt so much?

But there is nothing to be done now.

As the sun begins to appear above the mountains, Vanye comes upon a Chya patrol. He fights halfheartedly, like a man who feels no sweetness in life.

The Chya bury him in accordance with ritual, though one said such rites were too good for *ilinin*.

*Turn to Section 29.*

## * **11** *

Vanye slyly creeps up on the Koris Wolf. He notes with grim satisfaction that the beast's keen nose seems too intent on sniffing out Morgaine's wounded form to notice his approach.

Vanye raises the longsword, holds it high for a moment, and brings it down full on the Koris Wolf's broad back.

*For his surprise attack, Vanye gets a +3 to his attack roll and if he hits, does double damage. If the Wolf survives the surprise attack, it will attack in the next round. Vanye gets the first attack of the new round, as usual.*

**KORIS WOLF**
*To hit Vanye: 14   To be hit: 8   Hit Points: 8*
*Damage with claws   Damage with*
*and fangs: 1 D6+1   longsword: 2 D6*
*                    Damage with dagger: 1 D6*

*The Koris Wolf attacks with a ruthless savagery. It will fight until it kills or is killed.*

*If Vanye kills the Koris Wolf, turn to section 17.*

## Section 11

*If the wolf kills Vanye, turn to section 29.*

*If Vanye should turn and run away into the woods, turn to section 13.*

# * **12** *

*"Liyo,"* Vanye says. He waits to be acknowledged.

She looks at him, then gives him leave to speak. He gropes for the words.

"The horses, lady," he says. "They sense something nearby." Morgaine says nothing. "I do not think we are alone here," he adds.

Morgaine reins her horse to a stop. She looks at Vanye, and her gaze is so penetrating he wishes he had not spoken. At length she says, "If there is trouble, we had best be informed of it. Take a little time to scout on foot. See if thy fears are rightly grounded."

Vanye nods. He slips off his horse, and secures his weapons about him. He starts up the rocky defile. He can feel Morgaine's eyes on his back.

He steels cautiously along the rocky ledge above the narrow pass. From this vantage point he has a clear view of the blighted landscape below. The farmers who work this land are doubly cursed, he muses, to have mad leaders ruling above them, and twisted, frozen land below them.

Vanye sees a rustic farmhouse ahead, further

## Section 12

along the trail. Moving closer, he spies some activity in the courtyard. A half-dozen burly men in furs and armor busy themselves with placing all the meager household valuables in a sack, and smashing what little remains. The bodies of a family lie bloody in the snow.

Vanye notes grimly that from his vantage point he could fire four or five arrows at them before they could react and storm him. Still, he has no reason to seek trouble. Not without the consent of his *liyo*. He turns and heads back to her. On the way back, Vanye surveys the surrounding trails, and works out a path that will take them well around the trouble.

When Vanye reaches the spot where Morgaine is waiting, he tells her of the brigands. She listens impassively.

"We haven't time to stop and wait for them to leave," Morgaine says. "If they wish trouble, we can provide it aplenty. We will continue this way."

*If Vanye should beg that they re-route around the trouble, turn to section 23.*

*If Vanye should hold his tongue and continue to ride, turn to section 26.*

# * **13** *

Vanye turns and runs through the undergrowth, trying to put distance between himself and the huge beast. His heart races. In the distance he hears a savage snarl, and a woman's scream of pain. Then he hears a searing roar, and silence.

"*Ilin?*"

It was Morgaine's voice.

His throat stings as he thinks of the honor lost in leaving his *liyo*'s side in such a cowardly way. Better by far to die protecting her than to lose the last vestiges of honor.

*If Vanye should return to Morgaine in shame, turn to section 20.*

*If Vanye should take this opportunity to flee Morgaine's side, turn to section 10.*

# * **14** *

Vanye studies the strange *qujalin* equipment uneasily. To use such evil medicine may taint his soul. But his very situation as *ilin* to such a lord puts his soul in jeopardy.

"Yes, *liyo*. Do what you can."

Morgaine efficiently busies herself with her preparations. "Remove thy armor." she instructs. Vanye complies, revealing the gaping slashes left by the beast. He watches transfixed as Morgaine sprays a wet, pinkish film onto the wound. The film dries quickly.

Vanye feels the strange magics seep along his back. Pain flees from the wound, leaving a sickly sweet numbness. Vanye's face flushes with shame at being so weak as to willingly accept sorcery into his body. He feels sick at heart.

"What is wrong? Do the medicines pain thee?" she inquires, peering at him quizzically.

"It is nothing," he replies. He rises and walks to the edge of the firelight.

His watch is over before dawn.

Add *+6 to Vanye's Hit Points from the healing.*

*(Note that Vanye can never have more Hit Points than he starts with.)*

*Turn to section 22.*

# * **15** *

Vanye silently raises his sword and takes a cautious step forward. His foot disturbs the undergrowth. The huge Koris Wolf jerks its head around quickly and looks into Vanye's eyes. Its eyes are those of a madman and not an animal . . .

Vanye swings the sword and in the same instant the great wolf is upon him, spitting and snarling.

KORIS WOLF
*To hit Vanye: 13   To be hit: 9   Hit Points: 8*
*Damage with claws    Damage with*
*and fangs: 1 D6+1    longsword: 2 D6*
*Damage with dagger: 1 D6*

*The Koris Wolf attacks with a ruthless savagery. It will fight until it kills or is killed.*

*If Vanye kills the Koris Wolf, turn to section 17.*

*If the wolf kills Vanye, turn to section 29.*

*If Vanye should turn and run away into the woods, turn to section 13.*

# * 16 *

Taomen falls into a bloody heap, his sword slipping from his lifeless fingers. Vanye looks at the twisted body, and fears for what the Chya will do to him for this killing. And then, inexplicably, he feels a strange regret. It is as if killing Taomen has robbed him of his only chance to live in Ra-koris? But what chance did he ever have to live in Ra-koris? Why should he think such a thing?

Then the memories flood him. He feels himself sinking into them. For a single, crazed moment, Taomen's body becomes the bloody body of his brother Kandrys. Another killing in a friendly hall. Is this his fate, then? Is he doomed to kill all who give him aid? He shakes the evil thoughts away. People are spilling into the room, and warriors are circling him warily.

Vanye looks for an opening. There is a clear space behind and to the left of him. If he makes a break for it, he may be able to get to the stairs, find Morgaine and tell her of the attack and treachery.

A man's voice rings out. "Vanye!" the man shouts. It is Lorn. "You are among friends. Stop fighting, and you will not be hurt. I give you my

## Section 16

word on this. We do not hold this killing against you!"

Vanye considers this suspiciously, but keeps an eye on the other warriors.

*If Vanye should stop fighting and talk to Lorn, turn to section 32.*

*If Vanye should run and try to find Morgaine, turn to section 64.*

# * 17 *

Vanye looks at the bloodied carcass of the Koris Wolf. There was no honor in killing such a beast. Were it an honest beast he could at least feel regret. As it is he feels only disgust. Still, he has saved his wounded *liyo*, Morgaine. And there is honor in that, at least.

He returns to camp, cleaning his bloodied blade.

Morgaine is waiting for him, awake.

"I see thee has met with trouble, *ilin*," she says.

"A Koris Wolf," he replies. He sits and stares into the fire.

"Is something troubling thee, *ilin*?" she asks.

Had she read his mind? Is his mind and soul an open book to her? No, it can not be. Vanye refuses to accept that. She is merely wise in the ways of people.

He slowly nods. "The beast. The Koris Wolf. How does Thiye make such things?"

"He does not so much make them as draw them through," she replies. "He uses the gates to reach places where such things are normal, and brings them here, where they are not natural. Many die. But some live and breed. They are driving away all native life. If Thiye is not stopped, soon all the world will be as the Koris woods are now.''

Vanye shudders.

*If Vanye is wounded, turn to section 9.*

*If Vanye is not wounded, turn to section 22.*

# * 18 *

Vanye studies the great wolf for a moment. It is tempting to attack now, but that would insure a fight with the monstrous creature. The beast has not attacked yet, and perhaps will not attack at all. After all, fires keep away most wolves.

Keeping a watchful eye on the beast, Vanye carefully pads his way back to camp. He resumes his watch, but this time he is fully awake. He looks at the area where the wolf was, and sees a pair of wicked eyes glinting in the firelight. Vanye fixes a fierce gaze on the wolf, as if to say 'come no further. You don't frighten me.' The Koris Wolf blinks in surprise over having been spotted. It recovers its composure and glowers back at Vanye. The two lock gazes in an animalistic territorial struggle, both determined to make the other break first.

*Roll 3 D6 against Vanye's Wisdom. If the roll is less than or equal to Vanye's wisdom, he has stared the wolf down. Turn to section 86.*

*If the roll is greater than Vanye's Wisdom, Vanye fails the power struggle. Turn to section 88.*

# * **19** *

Vanye looks at the scribe in disbelief. "I cannot. On my honor I cannot. An *ilin* is not free to leave his master."

The scribe keeps blinking at Vanye, not comprehending that Vanye is turning down his offer. He tries thrusting the bag of silver at Vanye, wondering why Vanye does not take it. Vanye knocks it from the old man's hands. The coins scatter across the rotting hay. The old scribe backs away, through the door. Vanye hears voices muttering behind the door.

"Oh, must you?" the scribe's muffled voice says. "Oh, well. Try not to hurt him."

Four Leth warriors stalk in, two of them holding clubs, and two with nets. Vanye draws his sword.

"I am under the protection of this house," he says, backing up. The men continue stalking him. He looks around frantically for an exit. He sees a door off to the left. Reaching it would be a gamble, but looked possible.

*If Vanye should fight the men, turn to section 42.*

*If Vanye should flee, turn to section 58.*

## * **20** *

The camp is quiet when Vanye returns. The body of the huge Koris Wolf is stretched out across the cleared ground, its body locked in a leap. Its blank eyes stare out, as if in disbelief that it could die so easily and without a mark.

Morgaine is lying down on her bedroll. She is looking at him in the flickering glow of the dying firelight. Vanye does not meet her gaze. "*Ilin*," she says. Now he must look at her. He does so, and the shame he feels is overwhelming.

"Remove the carcass," she says.

He pulls the massive body of the wolf into the woods, and returns to the camp. She says nothing, but her silence cuts deeper than her words could. He had betrayed her. She would be entirely within her rights to demand his life . . .

Morgaine goes to sleep. Vanye resumes his watch.

*Turn to section 22.*

# * **21** *

From soothing darkness, the harsh light of pain
begins to pour into Vanye's mind. He notes,
without much enthusiasm, that he is still alive.
He smells moldy hay and damp, musty stone. A
stable. He feels rough hands moving him. Slowly he opens his eyes.

He is tied with stout rope, and is being placed
into a wagon. He is wearing his armor, and his
sword is next to him in the wagon. The stable
appears to be in one of the crumbling stone
halls of Leth, probably that of a lesser lord.
Vanye can tell from the pervading stench of
decay that he is in Ra-Leth.

An old man in the robes of a scribe is fussing
over three burly Leth bandit-warriors. The old
man says, "Now don't damage him! Hurry! We
must get to the Gate and back before the witch
realizes we are gone!" Two of the warriors help
the old man onto the wagon. The third cracks a
whip over the team of horses, and the wagon
lurches forward.

Vanye struggles to wriggle free of the ropes,
which were tied carelessly. The wagon rumbles
out the door of the stable, and into the cool
night air.

*Roll 3 D6 against Vanye's Strength. If the roll is equal to or less than Vanye's Strength, the ropes are stretched enough for Vanye to try to slip free of them. If the Strength roll was successful, roll 3 D6 against Vanye's Dexterity. If this roll is less than or equal to Vanye's Dexterity, Vanye has managed to wriggle out of the ropes that were tying him.*

*If Vanye succeeds in both rolls, he is free of the ropes, and can grab his sword and return to the hall and look for Morgaine. Turn to section 74.*

*If he fails either roll he squirms and thrashes helplessly in the back of the wagon during the journey. Turn to section 79.*

## * **22** *

The next morning Vanye and Morgaine ride northward again.

As they ride through a narrow defile, the horses seem skittish. Vanye looks at the way ahead, peering intently for some clue of what is shying the horses. His people have the greatest respect for their horses and prize a horse's instincts highly. So Vanye is puzzled and not a little worried when he sees nothing to account for the horse's uneasiness. Even the worst of the creatures that stalk the plains of Koris seldom venture out in daylight.

Vanye scrutinizes Morgaine, wondering if he dares interrupt her grim concentration to voice his suspicions.

*If Vanye should tell Morgaine of his suspicions, even though he has no real grounds for them, turn to section 12.*

*If Vanye should keep his suspicions to himself, turn to section 26.*

# * **23** *

"Lady," Vanye continues, aware of how close he is to impertinence before his *liyo*. "From the ledge I spotted a trail near the lake that will take us away from the farmhouse. It is over rocky land, and will take a little longer than our current path, but we can avoid the bandits altogether."

Morgaine studies him. "Very well," she says. "We will try thy rocky trail."

Vanye feels relieved.

He leads them up the rocky cliff. The going is hard on the horses, but soon they reach the trail Vanye had spotted. They ride eastward a ways, following the shore of Lake Domen. The ground continues to rise. The land they ride along grows increasingly twisted, and the rough trail grows more uneven. Vanye peers ahead, straining to make out the way. Then, with an ugly sinking sensation, Vanye realizes why the trail was so poorly kept up. He sees the standing stones.

Great pillars of unnatural perfection jut out of the still waters of the lake, and many smaller ones dot the surface of the water like stumps, as if an entire *qujalin* city is beneath the water. More monoliths dot the land around the lake, and at the top of a far hill stand two greater pillars.

"The *Gate of Koris-leth*," Morgaine says.

Vanye nods. Now he realizes why the area near the farm was so twisted and bleak. The Gates have made all honest life corrupt.

So why does he follow this woman, whose life's purpose was the Gates?

They ride past the hill where the Gate stands. Morgaine studies it. Vanye keeps his eyes on the broken road ahead.

"Vanye."

"Yes, *liyo*?"

"Do you see the shimmering field within the gate?"

Vanye reluctantly looks toward the Gate. "Yes, *liyo*," he says morosely.

"Does the shimmering appear to pulse?"

Vanye looks away. "Please, *liyo*, do not ask me. Such matters are beyond me."

Morgaine says nothing, but looks displeased. "Wait here," she says, after a time. She rides her magnificent gray up the bare little hill to the gate. She dismounts and studies the twin pillars, running her hand over their smooth surfaces and the ugly, blockish letters carved upon them. Vanye waits, cold and alone. At length she returns.

"Our plans have changed, *ilin*. There is a problem with this Gate that may make a trip to

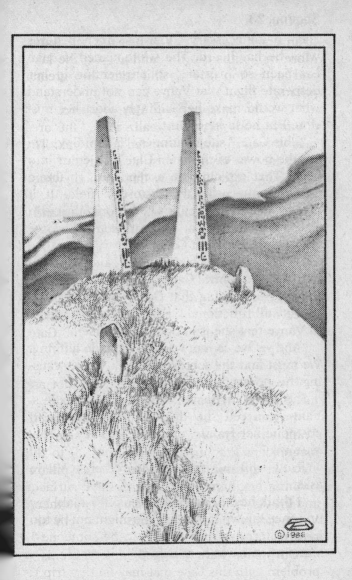
© 1986

Hjemur unnecessary." Vanye scarcely believes what he has heard. The white-maned woman has been so insistent, so unrelenting in her desperate flight that Vanye can not understand what would make her willingly abort her mission. But he says nothing.

"This Gate," she continues, "is rapidly drawing the power of the main Gate at Hjemur into itself. That explains the exceptional, rhythmic pulsing pattern in the distortion field. If it should take full power, it will become the main Gate, and the one at Hjemur would become merely a subservient Gate.

"If we continue on to Hjemur, and this Gate becomes the central Gate, our mission would be in vain. Destroying that Gate would leave the others still functional." For a moment it seems to Vanye that she is at odds with herself.

"And yet we cannot wait here and do nothing. We must find the sorcerer in Leth who is causing this power flux."

She looks distracted and suddenly restless. Vanye can tell she does not like having to postpone her frantic, obsessive journey to Hjemur.

"How will we find this sorcerer?" Vanye asks.

"I think he will wish to find us. If I make my presence known in Ra-Leth, he might not be too hard to ferret out. It may even be someone I knew when I was here before."

Her words chill him. "How . . . ?" he asks.

"The Gates can be used to keep one young. Sorcerers can use the power of the Gates to take the bodies of others, for their own, preserving their lives indefinitely. I won't recognize the body of the sorcerer, but he will likely be a strong, healthy man.

"They tend to take the bodies of warriors," she adds absently.

Vanye shudders. To have a *qujalin* sorcerer take over one's body was too horrible a fate to consider. One's soul would be destroyed surely. Vanye makes a sign to ward off evil, but it does not make him feel better.

They turn and ride toward Ra-Leth. Morgaine does not speak during the ride. At first Vanye is glad of it, but soon he begins to wish for some words from the grim woman. But of course voicing such desires is not acceptable behavior in *ilinin*, so Vanye accepts the silence. At least he is still alive, with his soul intact.

That evening a group of ten burly warriors in furs ride up to them, and demand that Morgaine ride with them to the keep of their master, Lord Grivvar. She graciously consents to accompany them.

The Leth warriors bring Morgaine and Vanye to a crumbling old stone fortress that stinks of mold and decay. They are led into the dank ruin, and swallowed by its darkness.

## Section 23

Morgaine leaves Vanye in the stables. "Tend the horses," she says softly. "I do not trust this household to do it. When you are done, join me." She leaves and Vanye sets to work, rubbing down the weary horses. He marvels at Siptah, Morgaine's magnificent gray. Such horses are now known only in legends spun by old Nhi warriors who spend most of their days dreaming of old battles and old glories.

As Vanye finishes currying the gray and begins on his own pony, a door creaks open, and an elderly scribe with a face like crinkled parchment enters. He hobbles over to Vanye and sits down on a bale of mouldy hay. Vanye waits for him to speak.

The old man thinks for a moment, as if trying to recall why he was there. Then he brightens, and stands up. He announces in a croaking voice, "His lordship Lord Grivvar has sent me to you with a message. He wishes you to leave Morgaine's service." Vanye is thunderstruck.

"In return he wishes to give you a large bag of silver coins." The old man smiles serenely and produces a heavy bag of coins.

Vanye is confused. "Why does he wish this?" he asks.

"You are a fine warrior, no? His lordship needs fine warriors."

"But I serve Morgaine . . ." he begins.

The scribe shakes his head. "Tut, tut," he intones gravely. "There is no future in it. Better to take my master's offer."

*If Vanye should accept the scribe's offer, turn to section 65.*

*If Vanye should reject the offer, turn to section 19.*

## * **24** *

Vanye violently pushes Morgaine's arm, disrupting her aim. She looks at him wildly.

He pays her no attention, but instead cries out "Chya cousins! We have no fight with you! Will you put kin-slaying on your souls?"

Stealthy shapes move among the trees. Then three green-clad bowmen step out of the woods. They are Chya, men of his mother's people. Two are tall, and the leader is short. All three are lean and rugged from their harsh hunter's life. Vanye bows low.

"I am Nhi Vanye i Chya, *ilin* to this lady, who is clan-welcome with Chya."

The leader studies Morgaine suspiciously. "And who is she?"

Vanye looks to Morgaine. She gives no answer. Damn her stubbornness, Vanye thought. Does she want to die here? Does she not know that the Chya bowmen could have them both feathered with cheery green arrows in seconds? She could have no possible defense against such things. Or could she?

The Chya were growing impatient. Vanye decides to risk the death he knows over the death he doesn't.

"She is Morgaine kri Chya," Vanye says. A tense murmur passes through the three bow-men, and from further in the woods, Vanye notes. He quickly adds over the tumult, "She has clan-welcome that was never withdrawn."

The men are visibly shaken. They were pre-pared for the madmen of Leth, and even unnat-ural beasts from Hjemur, but not for a sorceress one hundred years dead.

After brief discussion with his men, the leader says, "We will take you to Ra-koris. I am Tao-men." Morgaine gives a stiff, barely polite bow. She does not seem too pleased with this turn of events, but is willing to go along. Vanye allows himself to release his breath, which he suddenly realizes he has been holding.

Ra-koris of old was a magnificent stone hall, as splendid as the Chya themselves. But it was destroyed in the wars against Hjemur, and lay in ruins not far from the new hall. New Ra-koris is an earth-floored hall made of rough logs, that reflect the fall of a once mighty clan. The ruins of the old hall are grim and desolate, in contrast to the earthy life of the new.

The houses nearby are merely huts of brush and logs, but they have a warmth and charm that none of the old stone buildings in Leth can match. Women and children bustle about along-side the roads, and a few small animals run underfoot. The village is full of life and hope. It makes Leth look diseased, and even makes Vanye's austere home in Ra-morij seem slow and gray by comparison. It makes Vanye a little sad to think that the world of his mother's Chya people will be forever denied him.

They dismount before the main hall. A great many people turn out to see them, filling the huge hall almost completely. The crowd parts courteously to allow Morgaine and Vanye through. They study Morgaine with great interest.

The log hall of Ra-koris is impressive from the inside. It has two stories and many rooms. Though it is wood, it looks sturdy enough to withstand at least a brief siege. The hides of many beasts, natural as well as strange, decorate the walls and provide protection from the winds of winter. The hall is lit by smoky torches that are spaced along the length of the hall, and by a grand stone hearth, larger even than that in most halls of stone.

The bowmen leave them there to wait for Chya Roh, the lord of the Chya, Vanye's cousin. Chya Roh is likely to bear a grudge against Morgaine, as four thousand of the ten thousand men she had led to destruction at Hjemur had been of Chya. Roh is no more likely to bear good will toward Vanye. Vanye knows that Roh still pursues bloodfeud with his homeland—his former homeland—of Nhi, over the matter of Vanye's mother's abduction from Chya. Vanye is sure that Chya Roh would enjoy a chance to end this shame on his house. It is in Chya Roh's power to order Vanye's death, if he so desires it, as partial restitution for either crime. Vanye shudders and clutches his sword hilt for comfort.

Late in the day, Chya Roh enters the hall, flanked by a brace of warriors. He pays no attention to Vanye, to Vanye's infinite relief, and instead addresses Morgaine.

Chya Roh demands proof Morgaine is who she claims to be, and she regally presents him with the insignia of the old High Kings of Koris, which obligates the Chya to provide her with their hospitality.

After some discussion, Chya Roh relents, agreeing to give her the shelter she requests. Vanye relaxes a little after that, feeling slightly relieved.

As Roh is taking his leave, he finally deigns to look at Vanye. "You claim this?" he asks Morgaine. "You could do better, lady." He turns and leaves.

Morgaine is given a room on the upper floor, and Vanye is given a place by the hearth. He settles down, grateful for the chance to take off his armor. He luxuriates in the freedom his limbs feel once out of the confining mail.

But he does not have long to enjoy his comfort. Taomen comes to him and says, "Chya Lorn, Roh's brother wishes to speak with you."

Vanye feels panic. What treachery is this? To question *ilin* on his master's business was not honorable. And yet he cannot refuse a sum-

## Section 24

mons from the second-in-line to lordship over the Chya.

*If Vanye should go with Taomen, turn to section 67.*

*If Vanye should refuse to go, turn to section 53.*

## * **25** *

Vanye turns away from the *qujalin* equipment. "Do you command me as *ilin* to submit to this medicine?"

"No," she says quietly. "I will not force thee."

She looks at him for a long moment, then sinks back down onto her bedroll to rest.

Vanye kneels on his mat again to continue his watch. His limbs are weary, and his wounds pain him fiercely, but he feels a strange exhilaration. The feeling remains throughout his watch.

*Turn to section 22.*

# * **26** *

The two continue riding along the narrow pass. They come upon an area where the huge boulders obstruct their view of the land ahead, though there does appear to be a farmhouse in the distance.

Vanye's horse stiffens for a moment, and the pass erupts in madness. Men on horseback hurtle towards them, swords flashing. Men on foot slide down the rocky slopes behind them, and block their retreat. Morgaine draws her lesser blade, and continues charging, trampling and slicing the brigands.

BANDITS
*To hit Vanye: 12    To be hit: 11    Hit Points: 6*
*Damage with clubs:    Damage with longsword:*
*1 D6                          2 D6*

*                                 Damage with dagger:*
*                                 1 D6*

*There are seven bandits. Three will fight Vanye. The fight will last five combat turns. If Vanye takes more than 10 points of damage, he will be knocked unconscious by the clubs. If Vanye is not knocked unconscious within that time, the ban-*

dits will flee, and Vanye can take a parting shot at one. If Vanye kills all three brigands in less than five turns, the ones fighting Morgaine will flee.

If Vanye is killed, turn to section 29.

If Vanye is clubbed into unconsciousness, turn to section 21.

If Vanye drives off the bandits, turn to section 30.

# * **27** *

Vanye hears the clash of steel coming from the great hall. Morgaine is under attack. It is his duty to his *liyo* to keep her alive, even if it means countering a previous order. He can not bear to think of her facing so many armed men alone.

He runs back to the great hall. There is a ripping, roaring noise from within, as if a great wind is blowing into the room. Vanye trembles in fear, but strides in.

He is stunned by the sight that greets him. A great, opalescent, shimmering vortex roars through the room, and the stars seem to twinkle and whirl within it. At the base of the vortex is Morgaine, brandishing Changeling. From the unsheathed sword issues the black field, which hurls the warriors about, and sucks them crying and wailing into the starry black void.

Morgaine sees Vanye and cries out to him in desperation, but it is too late. The inky force grips Vanye and sends him hurtling into a violently cold maelstrom. The last thing he sees as he flies toward Morgaine is an unexplainable look of despair on her face.

*Turn to section 29.*

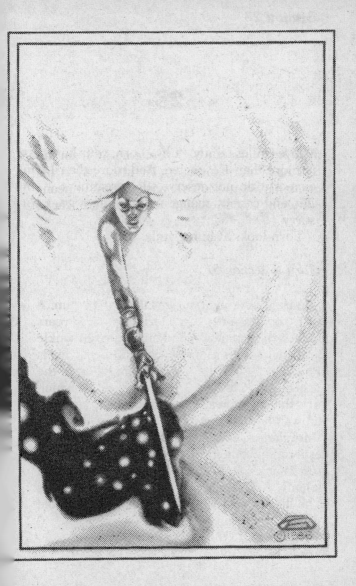

## * **28** *

Vanye smiles faintly. "Chya Lorn, your kindness is more than I expected. And more than I can expect. I do not deserve such treatment. I am *ilin*, and cannot change that. I cannot go. I am sorry."

Lorn looks at him grimly.

*Turn to section 51.*

# * 29 *

*This Adventure is over.*

*Vanye is slain or no longer able to aide his mistress. If you wish to, you can turn back to section 1 and begin again. Perhaps this time your judgment or luck with the dice will be better.*

# * **30** *

Without a backward glance, Morgaine rides away from the corpses of the bandits. She does not speak. Vanye follows, observing her apparent need for silence. Ahead, several ransacked farmhouses testify to the recent passage of the bandits.

The two ride on toward the mountains on the northern horizon. The day is quiet.

*Turn to section 35.*

# * **31** *

At first there was nothing but dark and calm. Then, far away, light crept in. Then sound. And then pain. Harsh glare and senseless gibbering. Vanye opens his eyes. He lies bound on a windswept hill. Two imposing monoliths loom above him. A Gate. The Witchfires of Leth. Numbing fear creeps over him. Strange noises float from the dark woods nearby.

Twenty men of Leth stand on the hill, shifting about nervously. Vanye notices three among them who were in the Chya hall. They'd been in disguise then. He curses himself for not having noticed how out of place they looked among the kindly, happy people of Ra-koris.

Chya Lorn steps over and looks down at Vanye. "Greetings," he says from the perverse light that shines in his eyes. Vanye can see he is mad.

"You are a fine specimen of a man," Lorn says. "I shall enjoy your body far more than this Chya body, or my former hobbled body as the scribe of Lord Grivvar of Leth." He pinches Vanye's arm, almost affectionately. "Indeed, I shall enjoy this body more than I have enjoyed a body for over two hundred years."

# Section 31

Vanye goes cold, and feels very afraid. "Why?" he whispers in shock. "Why do you do this?"

Lorn gives an ugly chuckle. "Morgaine's secrets, of course," he says. "With her knowledge, I can take over the power of the master Gate at Hjemur, and steal wicked old Thiye's darkness. My dream of darkness will flood the world, eclipsing his." He laughs softly. "In your body, I shall join Morgaine, and learn all."

Vanye laughs, loud and long, and as madly as Lorn. "Foolish man," he says. "Morgaine is long gone from here! She is likely halfway to Hjemur now! You will never join her."

Lorn smiles. "She will be back." And he pulls out Changeling. "We took it from her in Rakoris, while she slept a drugged sleep. She will come after it. I will arrange for her to 'rescue' you, or rather, me, and the blade will be restored to her."

Vanye feels a rush of self-hatred, as if he were responsible for this betrayal. His soul is in the greatest danger. He weeps bitterly. Lorn smiles a crooked smile, and walks away.

Lorn begins to manipulate the icons on the standing stones of the Gate, in preparation for the transfer. The men of Leth haul Vanye to his feet, and place him near the shimmering, pulsing field between the stones. Vanye struggles against the ropes. They begin to loosen, but not fast enough.

Lorn looks in Vanye's eyes, and Vanye feels a

## Section 31

jolt pass through him. His mind is aswirl, and the world turns upside-down.

First his body becomes numb, and then begins to feel alien sensations. . . . The last vestiges of his sanity crumble. He is seeing out of Lorn's eyes!

*Roll 3 D6 against Vanye's Constitution, to determine the results of the shock of the transfer on Vanye's nervous system.*

*If Vanye's Constitution is greater than or equal to the roll, turn to section 39.*

*If his Constitution is less than, turn to section 73.*

# * **32** *

Vanye relaxes from his warrior's stance, but remains wary. He moves toward his armor under Lorn's watchful eye. There is echoing silence in the great hall.

Lorn notices this, and says with a smile, "If you feel more comfortable in your armor, by all means, put it on." This surprises Vanye. He is expecting treachery, deceit, or even attack. But this . . . He hurriedly straps on his armor.

When Vanye is armored, Lorn says, "Come this way. We can talk in here." He leads Vanye into a small room off the main hall.

*Turn to section 41.*

# * **33** *

Miraculously, Vanye and Morgaine survive the fight, but at a cost. Vanye's horse has been slain outright. The bone of the right foreleg of Morgaine's magnificent gray is broken and juts sharply through badly shredded sinew. Vanye tries to quiet the horse's whimperings, and make it as comfortable as possible.

Morgaine draws the horse away from Vanye. He asks "Your *qujalin* medicines? Can they . . ." but her look answers his question. She leads the limping horse a few paces away, utters strange words too softly for Vanye to hear, and then draws her smaller blade along Siptah's throat. The mighty horse bucks, as blood spurts from the deep slash in its throat, then he lies still.

They take as much of their equipment as they can carry off the horses' bodies, bury the rest, and set off into the evening.

The next Chya patrol they come across does not do them the kindness of firing a warning shot. When the final arrow fells him, Vanye struggles to see if Morgaine fights on. But he does not have the strength to turn far enough to face her. He notes with some surprise that his last thoughts are not on the state of his soul, but of Morgaine, and his sorrow at failing her.

*Turn to section 29.*

# * 34 *

At length Vanye speaks. "Chya Lorn, I thank you for the kindness you have shown me. I do not understand why you wish to be kind to me. I feel unworthy of such kindness. But I cannot break oath."

"Vanye, debts are only binding between humans! You know that!"

"I do not know that she is not human," Vanye says softly. "As long as there is a doubt, I cannot leave her."

"Vanye, you are a fool!"

Vanye nods slowly. "Yes," he says. "I may be."

"Oh, that is your Nhi side talking! She leads you to certain death! Or worse! Don't you wish to leave her?"

Vanye does not answer. He averts his eyes from the young lord's face.

"Vanye?" Lorn continues, more insistently. Vanye turns away. Lorn grabs Vanye's arm and wrenches it. "Listen to me," he shouts viciously.

Saying nothing, Vanye slowly returns his gaze to Lorn's scowling face. Lorn then checks himself, forcibly turning his anger away from Vanye, and back into himself.

"Please," he says. His voice softens, but there is still an edge in it. "I know she is not human. I can give you proof sufficient that she is not human. Will you go with me and let me prove what I say is true? Or do you wish to stay with her?" he adds coldly.

Vanye thinks for a moment. "How can you prove she is *qujalin*?"

"In the ruins of old Ra-koris, there are still records and books. They were abandoned long ago, in the fall of that place. We have no leisure for books now. But the records that lie there describe all that is Morgaine, and they explain it beyond any doubt."

Lorn pauses a moment as Vanye considers this. Then he continues, "The ride will take but a few hours, and you will be back before she even knows you are gone. You have nothing to lose, cousin, and the most vital knowledge to gain."

"Lorn, I am *ilin*—"

"So you are fond of saying. What of it?"

"I cannot leave without her permission."

"Oh? Well, consider it a decree from the lords of this house that you go with us. While she is here she must abide by our laws. And besides, you do not need her permission for a mere tour of the grounds."

*If Vanye should go with Lorn to old Ra-koris, turn to section 49.*

## Section 34

*If Vanye should insist on getting permission from Morgaine before he goes, turn to section 61.*

*If Vanye should refuse to go at all, turn to section 28.*

# * **35** *

There is a flash of green, and an arrow strikes the ground between their horses. A Chya arrow. A miss from the most renowned bowmen in the land? It must be a warning. Though Vanye is not welcome in Chya land, he is of half Chya blood, and knows their ways.

In an instant, Morgaine has her bow out and aimed. Vanye is close enough to keep her from firing. If he lunges at her he could stop her bowshot before she starts a fight.

*If Vanye should try to stop Morgaine from firing, and try to reason with the Chya while the Chya still aren't aiming at them, turn to section 24.*

*If Vanye should draw his bow and join the fight, turn to section 40.*

* **36** *

Vanye fights like a man possessed, driving back some of the warriors who fight him, and filling them with fear. But in the end, the odds against him are too great. The burly Chya men subdue him with their clubs, beating him until the room swirls around him, and everything is drenched in a blood-red haze.

Lorn leers down at him, and pinches Vanye's cheeks, saying, "Yes, I can use this well." Then he notices the growing lump on Vanye's skull, and cuffs one of the men. "Fool!" he shouts. "This is going to hurt me!"

As Vanye slips into unconsciousness, he is aware of being hauled outside.

*Turn to section 31.*

# * 37 *

The first thing Vanye feels are the soft sheets. He has not slept in a real bed since his exile from Ra-morij two years ago. He thinks he is dreaming. Dreaming that he is home, that he never killed his half-brother. All is well. He begins to relax, sinking luxuriously into the softness of the bed. Then he realizes he is in a Chya hall, and suddenly all tranquility flees like morning mist.

He is gripped by a gnawing terror. The Chya are his enemies. Chya Roh, leader of the Chya, bears a special grudge against Vanye, for Vanye is the result of the rape of Roh's own aunt. Even without that they have every reason to wish to seek Vanye's death. He attacked their men in the woods. Attacked them and lost. So why is he still alive?

There is a gentle rap on the door, and a short Chya warrior enters. "I am Taomen," he says curtly. "Chya Lorn, brother of Chya Roh wishes to speak with you."

Alone and without weapon and armor, Vanye has no choice but to comply.

## Section 37

*The Chya have bound Vanye's wounds. Return 2 d6 hit points to his current total.*

*Turn to section 41.*

## * **38** *

With the skill of a master Nhi horseman, Vanye carefully eases his horse away from the warriors, and rides in closer to Lorn. He controls the beast so deftly and so casually that he appears to be doing nothing but riding forward; that the horse moved sideways on its own whim. The men riding with him pay no attention to Vanye as he leans in toward Lorn.

"Lorn," Vanye says quietly.

"Yes, cousin?"

"Are your men truly Chya?"

"Do they not seem so?"

"No. They do not."

"Ah, well, you have my word they are of Chya. Perhaps some illegitimacy in their family lines." He laughs softly, but uneasily.

Vanye leans closer to Lorn and points to one of the men. "I saw that one in Leth. He is a bandit warrior."

Lorn looks surprised. "You are sure of this?" he asks.

Vanye nods. The warriors still pay them no attention.

Lorn strokes his chin thoughtfully and worriedly. He glances furtively from Vanye to the men and back. At length he levels a cold eye at Vanye and says, "You are more resourceful than I thought. You are truly a superb candidate. Ah, well. Alas, I was hoping you would ride most of the way to Leth under your own power."

Vanye had his sword drawn in an instant, but before he can swing, one of the burly warriors leaps from his horse onto Vanye. They tumble into the dirt and wrestle. Leaves crackle and dry sticks break under them as they roll along the ground. The two other warriors dismount and walk over to join the fight, but do not draw weapons.

From high on his horse, Lorn imperiously barks orders. "Careful there!" he shrieks. "For god's sake don't damage him! I don't wish to feel pain in my new body!"

*Roll 3 d6 against Vanye's Strength for each of the three men. If all three of the rolls are less than or equal to Vanye's Strength, Vanye can leap on his horse and flee. If any one roll is greater than Vanye's Strength, Vanye has been subdued.*

*If Vanye wins the struggle, turn to section 52.*

*If Vanye loses the struggle, turn to section 31.*

## * **39** *

Vanye clutches his last shreds of sanity with what vestiges of honor his soul has left. He wants to run, he wants to hide, to bury himself in a dark and quiet place where such obscenity cannot affect him. It would be so easy to let his honor fade. Give in to peace. Fade . . .

No! Anything is preferable to that. He can not surrender his soul to sorcery. The thought repulses him so greatly that he struggles to claw his way out of the dark place his will has sunken into. It seems almost impossible: like climbing an icy, windswept cliff, but he continues.

With an eerie roaring in his ears that rattles through his bones, he finds his senses returning. His vision begins to clear. He sees his own bound body before him, the face leering, in the way that Lorn had. Lorn is in Vanye's body! The men of Leth are loosening the bonds on Vanye's body.

Vanye looks about wildly, and sees he appears to be Lorn. He's caught in the body of the man who is known as the second most powerful man in Ra-koris. Where is the real Lorn now?

## Section 39

Trapped in the same dark oblivion of madness that had been intended for Vanye?

But to be Lorn! It is agonizing, humiliating. If he is no longer himself he is helpless. And then he sees Changeling at his side, and wild hope floods over him.

*If Vanye should draw Changeling and use its power on Lorn (Vanye's body), turn to section 78.*

*If Vanye should draw Changeling and use its power on himself (Lorn's body), turn to section 75.*

*If Vanye should draw Changeling and use its power on the Gate, turn to section 68.*

*If Vanye should decide not to risk his soul by using Changeling, turn to section 94.*

## * **40** *

Vanye draws his bow, quick as lightning. He notches an arrow and lets it fly toward a shadow moving behind a tree. He and Morgaine fire frenetically at the stealthily moving shapes in the woods. A flurry of green-feathered arrows rain back upon them, as if the trees themselves are attacking.

CHYA BOWMEN
*To hit Vanye: 7   To be hit: 13   Hit Points: 9*
*Damage with bows:   Damage with longsword:*
*1 d6+2            2 D6*
            *Damage with bow:*
            *1 D6+2*

*There are six Chya bowmen. Three will fire at Morgaine, and three will fire at Vanye. The Chya did not wish a fight, but since Morgaine and Vanye have attacked, they have to fight back. However, they still wish to talk to Morgaine and will take her alive, if possible. If Vanye takes 8 or more points of damage without dropping below 0, he will pass out from rapid blood loss and the Chya will take him and Morgaine prisoner.*

## Section 40

*If Vanye and Morgaine win the fight, turn to section 33.*

*If Vanye passes out, turn to section 37.*

*If Vanye dies, turn to section 29.*

## * **41** *

"Cousin Vanye," Lorn begins, smiling serenely. "I am pleased to see you in Ra-koris."

Vanye starts. He had expected interrogation, anger, spite. Not a warm greeting.

Lorn chuckles, sensing Vanye's surprise. "Not all of us in Ra-koris share Roh's hatred of you for your Nhi blood. What happened to your mother, my aunt, was not your fault, and you should not have to pay the cost of it. She was a good woman, and did not deserve the contempt many Chya felt for her."

Vanye feels disoriented, but happy. He says, "I did not expect . . . friendship."

"Vanye, we are family. If you are an honorable man, your Nhi blood shall not be an obstacle with me. Even Roh can be made to see your worth."

Vanye nods, dazed by this unexpected turn of events.

"Of course, there is the matter of this . . . woman you serve. Roh fears her, and will not take kindly to you for being in her presence. Why do you follow her?"

Vanye's mouth goes dry. He feels all his good fortune draining away. Because of her.

## Section 41

Morgaine.

"I have no choice but to follow her. I am *ilin* to her," he says.

"Do you serve her willingly?"

Vanye thought for a moment. "It was a fair Claiming. I am in her debt."

Lorn's eyes twinkled. "So you think now," he says enigmatically. "There is an honest and rightful way out of your servitude. A way that puts no danger on your soul, and will restore your honor."

Vanye is shocked. He can not speak. Finally he says, "Do you speak truly?"

Lorn nods. "On my honor, and on the honor of my house, I do."

"Please," says Vanye. "If you know something I do not, pray speak!"

Lorn's happy eyes narrow coldly. "Tell me, Nhi Vanye i Chya. What is her mission?"

*If Vanye should answer truthfully in hopes of being told how to regain his honor, turn to section 55.*

*If Vanye should refrain from answering, even if at the risk of never being told how his honor may be restored, turn to section 63.*

# * **42** *

Vanye can see that the men are without honor. They have no compunctions against attacking a guest, against breaking with the most sacred of traditions. Despite being Leth, they ostensibly have honor, and it means nothing to them. Vanye feels no sympathy or mercy for such men. He spits out an oath and whips out his sharp longsword. He sends it screaming through the air, swinging in anger at the men in furs. They step back a pace, taken by surprise at Vanye's sudden savagery, and feeling just slightly foolish about facing a man with a sword while armed only with a net.

## LETH WARRIORS
*To hit Vanye: 13  To be hit: 9  Hit Points: 6*
*Damage with clubs:  Damage with longsword:*
*1 D6+1  2 D6*
*Damage with hands:*
*1 D6−2*

*The four men will try to capture Vanye with the net rather than fight him. While two attack with clubs, two will try to net him. Roll 3 D6 for the men with the net. If they roll above 8, they have*

## Section 42

netted him. If they succeed in netting him, the next round Vanye must roll under his Dexterity to escape the net, during which time he cannot attack. If the men keep him netted for two turns, Vanye cannot escape. Vanye may surrender at any time if he is rapidly losing hit points and prefers taking his chances to dying.

If Vanye wins the fight, turn to section 74.

If Vanye is netted or surrenders, turn to section 77.

If Vanye should run and flee, turn to section 58.

If Vanye dies in the fight, turn to section 29.

# * **43** *

Vanye dismisses the unformed fears in his mind with a shake of his head. Whatever the outcome, he will see it through. But he does desire to know more. So he shifts his attention to what Lorn is saying.

Lorn had been speaking all during Vanye's reverie, and Vanye has missed most of what Lorn has been saying. Lorn is currently talking of Chya patrols.

"We have managed to keep the Leth further south than last year. They are learning to respect our borders," the young lord was saying.

"Lorn," Vanye begins, barely waiting for the other man to finish speaking.

Lorn pauses a moment, evidently unaccustomed to being interrupted. A look of irritation flashes across his face momentarily, but he fights it back. "Yes?" he asks.

"You told me Morgaine is not human," Vanye continues softly. "If she is not human, what is she?"

Lorn laughs a nervous chuckle. "Oh, that would be hard to explain to one unaccustomed to *qujalin* sorcery."

"Then how is it you know of it?" Vanye asks pointedly.

# Section 43

Lorn stops laughing. He coughs sharply. "Er, Vanye, you do not seem to understand me."

"No," Vanye agrees.

"You see, Vanye, the sort of creature she is cannot be readily described. Not in simple terms." Lorn is not quite as cheerful as he had been a moment ago.

"Then how can this evidence in old Ra-koris convince me?" Vanye asks.

Lorn says nothing, but sits up straight in the saddle, summoning his full authority, and levels an imperious glare at Vanye. "Do you not trust me, Nhi Vanye?"

Vanye reflexively yanks his sword hand from the reins to his sword hilt, as if a hidden part of him suddenly senses danger. When he realizes what he is doing, he sheepishly brings his hand back to the reins and grips them tightly, hoping no one has taken notice of his action.

"I only wish to know the truth," Vanye says earnestly. "I hear so much from so many that I scarcely know what to believe. If you know something I do not, I beg you tell me."

"Yes," the young Lord says coldly. "I do know something you do not. I know much that you do not." His eyes look far away for a moment, as if he is seeing conflicts long gone. In that moment, it seems to Vanye that Lorn's eyes were those of a man who has seen much of sorrow and power; far more than his years would attest.

While staring fixedly into the distance, Lorn says in a strained, measured voice. "There are great beasts in this land; monsters that make the beasts in Koris look like barnyard fowl. The Witchfires brought them, the Witchfires keep them, and the Witchfires can make them from ordinary men."

Vanye shivers, more at the coldness and the distance in Lorn's voice than at what the man is saying.

"They command great forces. They influence the destinies of lords. And they deceive the innocent." Lorn's gaze snaps back from the far distance, and he levels his narrow, slitted eyes directly at Vanye. "Your Morgaine is one such monster. And you are one such innocent. I offer you freedom from her yoke. Do you still not trust me?" he asks severely.

Vanye's every instinct of self preservation bids him to hold his tongue, to cease provoking the lord's anger further. But part of him will not let the matter die. Perhaps it is that part of him that had defied his father's unfair command to kill himself. He quietly says, "I wish to know how the proof at Ra-koris is to convince me."

The warriors riding with them stop staring dully ahead, and turn furtive eyes toward Lorn. Vanye thinks he can see fear in those looks.

Lorn reins his horse to an abrupt stop. The others stop as well. For a frantic moment, Vanye considers fleeing, but he holds his ground.

Lorn levels a steely eye at him. There is a long pause, and Vanye can hear his own heart beat.

"Very well, Vanye," Lorn says. "Morgaine is

an ancient *qulajin* creature whose youth is sustained by the sorcery of the Witchfires. How do you think she survived the one hundred years since she destroyed the ten thousand?"

"She was caught in the world between," Vanye replies, "and time did not pass for her . . ." Vanye stops. He does not know how much Morgaine wished others to know.

"She told you that? And you believed her?" Lorn says. "More likely she was traveling about the world, taking the bodies of others."

"Then why would she look the same now as she did then?" Vanye asks.

Lorn takes a long breath. The warriors shift nervously on their horses, saddle leather creaking uneasily beneath their bulk.

"When we reach Ra-koris you will understand all," Lorn spits. "All!" He kicks his mount viciously in the ribs and spurs it along the trail.

Vanye watches him go. The warriors approach him menacingly, and he rides on after Lorn, his mind more full of questions than before.

They ride in silence a long way.

After a time, Vanye begins to feel disoriented, as if he isn't sure where they are going. At length he breaks the strained silence and says, "Lorn, how much farther is it?"

Lorn smiles a cold smile and says, "We shall be there in a moment. I am as eager to be there as you."

Vanye feels vaguely disconcerted by this, but

there is still no problem he can identify. He continues on.

Soon he sees the single jagged tower of old Ra-koris jutting above the tree line. It is the only portion of the old keep still standing. The rest had been razed, and now stands in ruins.

Lorn looks relieved to be here, and squirms happily in his saddle. He leads the men off the road and into a clearing. Ahead is the ancient ruin of Ra-koris. Huge stone blocks and columns are strewn about the interior, and burnt timbers scrape against the sky like an immense, broken ribcage. The one tower cuts defiantly into the night sky. The remains of the other towers are barely discernible amidst the rubble. A twenty foot wall rings the whole camp, though it is breached in places with immense holes.

Lorn pauses a moment, studying the place. "Here, Vanye," he says. Here you will have full proof of the sorcerous magics I told you of."

He motions with his hand, and the warriors silently follow him in. Vanye rides with them.

As they cross the threshold, Vanye shudders. The ruins have a forbidding air, and he feels as if his presence there is somehow defiling the sleep of the ancient stones. Still, it was made by men's hands, and is not a foul *qujalin* ruin.

Deep shadows fill most of the ruins, and the ground is treacherous. Several times Vanye's horse loses its footing. Then the beast shies. Vanye reins to a halt to see what is troubling the horse. From deep in the ruins he hears a horse whinny and stamp. He quickly reins around to ride the other way, but a dozen Leth warriors on horseback begin to close in behind Vanye and Lorn. Twenty more emerge from the gloom in front of them. Vanye looks to Lorn for help. For Leth to harm Lorn would invite serious Chya reprisals. And at the least, Lorn's ransom would be far greater than his own.

Lorn backs away from him, saying to the men of Leth, "Please take him gently. I do not wish to feel undue pain when I take his body."

Vanye feels his heart leap into his mouth. He knows all is lost, and he curses himself for falling into such a trap. He has almost no chance fighting against so large a group, and he sees no avenue of escape. If he surrenders, he might live. But then, would he not be better dead than suffering whatever foul *qujalin* rites Lorn has planned?

In his mad panic, he hears his father's voice, commanding him to fall on his own blade, to die an honorable death for killing Kandrys. He could not do it then, and so he was doomed to a life as an honorless *ilin*. Could he do it now?

The men close in on him slowly.

*If Vanye should fight, turn to section 50.*

*If Vanye should surrender, turn to section 57.*

*If Vanye should try to flee, turn to section 85.*

*If Vanye should kill himself, turn to section 62.*

# * **44** *

Vanye's sword is in his hand in an instant, and he begins to rain merciless blows on the traitorous Chya. He wades through their ranks, fighting like a man possessed. Blood trails in crimson arcs behind his blade, as the sword rises and falls, rises and falls on the bodies of his enemies. Their armor splinters before his onslaught, and his sword begins to bite deeply into the soft flesh beneath it.

One man falls back in fear. Vanye strikes him a contemptous blow that sends him crashing to the floor, clutching a bloody arm wound. Another burly Chya warrior charges forward, and impales himself on Vanye's sword. The warrior stares at Vanye for a moment in disbelief. Then the light fades from his eyes, and he slumps to the floor. Vanye struggles to remove his sword from the man's gut. The third warrior sees Vanye occupied with the dying man, and rushes forward, attacking Vanye while he's still trying to detach the warrior's corpse from his sword.

To avoid the attack, Vanye swings his sword, corpse and all, at the third warrior. The warrior's club bounces off the dead man's head, and Vanye wrenches his sword free.

## Section 44

Sweat breaks from the last Chya Warrior's brow, as he stares at Vanye's bloodied form. The warrior begins to back away, trying to escape the bloodlust in Vanye's eyes. He holds his club up before him, as if to warn Vanye away from closing with him. As he staggers backward, the warrior backs into one of the rough-hewn wooden columns that support the ceiling. He whirls around, expecting to see a new foe. Vanye closes, knocking the larger man's club away with a single slash across the man's arm.

The man sinks to his knees in horror, looking up at Vanye plaintively. Slowly, almost reverently, Vanye brings his sword down and splits the man's skull.

As the last of the three warriors fall dead at Vanye's feet, Chya Lorn turns white and flees the room. Vanye bolts after him, dripping blood along the wooden flooring. Lorn shouts strange oaths and heads directly toward a group of warriors who are sitting in the flickering light of many torches. Vanye curses and gives up the chase, running in another direction.

The sleepy hall begins waking up, roused by Lorn's shouts. Vanye heads up the wooden stairs. He runs from room to room, hoarsely calling Morgaine's name. Curious children poke their heads out at him.

"Thee has set the house astir."

Vanye nearly jumps when he hears Morgaine's calm voice behind him. He falls to his knees.

"Forgive me lady. They did attack me. They wished to wrest me from your service. I know not why."

"Roh?" she asks.

"Lorn."

"How curious. Is he dead?" Vanye shakes his head regretfully.

"Get thee up, *ilin*," she says. "We have company."

Vanye turns around. Roh is stalking up the stairs, flanked by a dozen warriors. There is fury in his eyes. Lorn is nowhere in sight. Vanye's heart pounds in his chest.

"Morgaine!" Roh thunders. "Your wretched excuse for a servant has killed three men!"

"Has he? Three men? By himself? Then he does not sound quite so wretched to me." She grins slightly as she says it, her eyes half-closed. In the soft torchlight Vanye thinks she looks almost beautiful.

"*Ilin!*" she snaps. "Why did thee do this thing which they accuse thee of?"

"Forgive me lady, they attacked me. I only sought to defend myself."

"Who ordered the attack?" she asks.

"Roh's brother, Lorn."

Roh scowls. "Why would he waste good steel on a half-blood Nhi bastard?" he sneers.

"He wished me to leave Morgaine's service," Vanye answers earnestly.

"I do not believe you!" snaps Roh.

Morgaine speaks again, calmly, soothingly.

## Section 44

"Why don't we find Lorn? Mayhap he can explain my servant's rash actions."

Roh thinks this over, looking coldly at Morgaine. At length he relents. He turns to one of his warriors and says, "Fetch Lorn here. We shall soon see who speaks with honor and who does not." The warrior runs down the stairs, calling for Lorn. Soon the household is awakened, and many people join the search. But Lorn is nowhere to be found.

Roh is furious. In a rage he tracks down the last person to have seen Lorn that evening. It is one of the group of warriors Lorn had run toward while being chased by Vanye. The warrior tells Roh: "Lorn sent us to chase Morgaine's *ilin*. He did not join the chase, but ran outside."

Roh scowls again. "What men did the *ilin* kill?"

The bodies of the slain men are brought out of the room where Vanye had fought them. After a brief inspection, one man cries out, "These are not our brothers! They are men of Leth!"

A great roar goes up in the hall. People stare in disbelief. Roh says coldly, "Why would men of Leth wish to serve Lorn?"

"Perhaps," says Morgaine, "he was not Lorn at all. Roh, where has your brother been these last days?"

Roh looks at her suspiciously. "With our patrols on our southern border, fighting the men of Leth. I did not know he had returned."

"Chya Roh," Morgaine says quietly. "I'd venture a guess that your brother has not come back."

Roh steps toward her, menacingly, as if he fears what she would say next.

"Your brother is likely dead and the person who attacked my *ilin* was a probably a creature of sorcery from Leth."

Roh is stunned. "You have been deceived, Roh." She continues: "And in your delusion you have insulted my servant and me. To make recompense for your affronts on my *ilin*, you will give me warriors to escort me as far as your northern border."

Roh is speechless, but he nods agreement.

Soon Vanye and Morgaine reach Hjemur, where they destroy the Gates, and end Thiye's evil rule there. And when Morgaine steps through the Gate to the world on the other side, Vanye follows.

*The Adventure has reached its end.*

# * **45** *

When Vanye can finally speak, he finds himself laughing. He feels slightly afraid, but his joy is far greater than his fear. "Chya Lorn, if you are sincere, and I am out of my debt to Morgaine, I thank you. It is as if my life were beginning again."

"In a way," Lorn says with a twinkle in his eye, it is. Come with me."

He leads Vanye along the rustic halls of new Ra-koris. The modest wood of the hall seems to glow with a warm life of its own in the reddish torchlight. Lorn brought Vanye to a room where they join three burly Warriors in Chya Buckskin.

"We shall escort you to your estate," Lorn says cheerfully. Vanye turns to him, staring blankly. "Oh, I neglected to tell you," Lorn adds, with an enigmatic smile. "You need not start as a landless warrior. We wish to title you with your own estate. It is not large, but is on very good land. Very near the site of Old Ra-koris. You will like it. Come."

"Should I not tell Morgaine first?"

Lorn looks at Vanye in disbelief. "Cousin Vanye, you owe her nothing. The woman is a force of evil. Her rage upon hearing will be implacable. For your own safety, we shall hide you. Come. We go to your estate, where you will be safe.''

*If Vanye should leave with Lorn, turn to section 49.*

*If Vanye should personally tell Morgaine he is out of her service, turn to section 54.*

# * **46** *

Taomen swings his sword violently at Vanye. Vanye frantically tries to dodge the blow. The little man is fully armored, and has a sword. Vanye is unarmored, and his sword is across the room from him.

**TAOMEN**
*To hit Vanye: 8   To be hit: 13   Hit Points: 10*
*Damage with sword:   Damage with longsword:*
*2 D6                          2 D6*
*                               Damage with hands:*
*                               1 D6−2*

*Vanye begins the fight barehanded. If he wants to make a desperate grab for his sword, Taomen gets a free attack at Vanye, and Vanye cannot get a return blow during that combat turn. To determine if Vanye successfully grabs his sword, roll Vanye's Dexterity on 3 D6. If the roll is less than Vanye's dexterity, he has the sword. If the roll is greater than Vanye's dexterity, he missed the sword. Vanye can try for as many turns as he wishes to get his sword, but in each turn he forfeits his attack.*

*If Vanye is killed, turn to section 29.*

*If Vanye kills Taomen, turn to section 16.*

*If Vanye reaches 5 hit points or less without going below 0, he has been knocked unconscious. Turn to section 31.*

# * **47** *

Without warning, Vanye draws his sword and savagely strikes at one of the men of Leth. The others shout curses and draw their clubs. In a panic Lorn turns his horse toward the woods and disappears in the thick undergrowth, shouting, "Do not hurt his body overmuch, or I'll have your souls!"

The three burly men close on Vanye, mad grins on their faces, and glints of desperation in their eyes.

**BURLY CHYA WARRIORS**
*To hit Vanye: 12   To be hit: 9   Hit Points: 8*
*Damage with clubs:   Damage with longsword:*
*1 D6+1                      2 D6*
                                 *Damage with hands:*
                                 *1 D6−2*

*The men will fight to subdue. If Vanye drops below 1 hit point, he is unconscious and captured.*

*If Vanye wins, turn to section 71.*

*If Vanye loses, turn to section 31.*

*If Vanye runs, turn to section 52.*

# * **48** *

Vanye's horse slams into Lorn's horse, spilling both riders onto the ground. Vanye braces himself and rolls with the fall. The impact rocks through his aching body and disorients him, but he fights the pain and staggers to his feet. Lorn hits the ground hard, and curls into a little ball like a man unaccustomed to fighting. Vanye looks at the Chya Lord in disgust. He has seen young children with more bravery.

He feels a wild urge to kill Lorn while he is helpless, but the sound of the approaching warriors forces him to change his mind. He moves toward his horse, but one of the warriors has already grabbed the reins and is leading it away from Vanye.

In panic, Vanye turns to run for the safety of the woods. Two riders close in on him, blocking his retreat. He dashes back to Lorn, hoping to hold him as a hostage. It is a dishonorable plan, but no more dishonorable than the imposter's.

The other mounted warrior gallops toward Vanye, cutting him off from Lorn's body. The warrior brandishes his club menacingly. A chill passes through Vanye; a strange feeling that this

## Section 48

is to be his last fight. He stands frozen for a moment, and in that instant is savagely struck down by one of the riders.

*Turn to section 31.*

## * **49** *

"Yes, of course you are right," Vanye says. "It would be foolhardy to tempt her wrath."

"Aye," says Lorn, nodding. "These inhuman creatures are given to flights of anger that destroy everything in their wake." He places a brotherly hand on Vanye's shoulder. "Get your horse and let us be on our way."

Vanye rides out into the darkness in the company of Lorn and three burly Chya warriors. The night air is particularly fragrant outside new Ra-koris. The ride takes Vanye, Lorn and the three warriors through rustic meadows and valleys. Lorn speaks pleasantly, and the warriors hold their tongues.

"I'm certain you will like your new estate," Lorn says. "It is on a rich piece of land. In a week's time we will hold the initiation ceremony to make you one of our own. Some of our more tradition-bound warriors may make reference to your Nhi heritage, and the unfortunate circumstances of your getting, but such trifles can be overcome by a word from me. And as for Chya Roh, well, I'm sure he will come to see your worth quite soon."

## Section 49

Lorn's words are pleasant and calming, but somehow they do not serve to reassure Vanye. He feels more anxious and edgy as time goes on. He tries to calm himself by listening to Lorn's soothing voice.

And yet something keeps bothering Vanye. Something feels out of place. Vanye dismisses the feeling. No doubt it is just some nagging uncertainty over whether he has betrayed Morgaine. Surely he has not. She is an inhuman creature who has no true claim to his service. One cannot betray one who is not human. And Morgaine is surely not human. Lorn has told him so. But what if Lorn is wrong?

He winces at the thought, and puts it out of his mind.

But something keeps buzzing around in the back of his mind. A small, quiet part of him is trying to tell him that something is wrong. He peers at Lorn, who is still happily chattering, but he can see nothing wrong.

*(Note—if Vanye did not have his weapons and armor in the preceding encounters, Lorn graciously allowed him to retrieve them before the ride. For future encounters, he is armored.)*

*Subtract 1 from Vanye's Wisdom, and roll 3 D6. If the roll is less than or equal to Vanye's Wisdom minus one, he has succeeded in figuring out what was bothering him. If the roll is greater than his Wisdom minus one, he has not worked it out.*

*If Vanye makes the roll, (rolls less than his wisdom) turn to section 56.*

*If Vanye fails to make the roll, (rolls more than his wisdom) turn to section 82.*

# * **50** *

Vanye draws his sword, shouts a war cry, and charges the nearest man of Leth. His sword bites deeply into the warrior's head, and the man falls from his horse, trailing blood.

Vanye swings again, and another man goes down . . . and another. The men of Leth strike at him with clubs.

The first blows are all but ineffectual, but soon they become a regular torrent, raining down on Vanye.

Vanye slips from his horse and falls into oblivion.

*Turn to section 31.*

# * 51 *

Lorn studies Vanye carefully, disappointment on his face. Then he speaks, "It pains me to have to do this. It pains me more than you know. If you will not come with me of your own will, you must be forced."

Vanye tenses, expecting trouble.

Lorn rises, and motions wearily. Three burly men in Chya buckskin step into the room from behind a heavy curtain. They are armed with heavy clubs.

Vanye cautiously backs to the door, but the men are on him before he reaches it. The only exit is blocked. The only way out is through the warriors.

Out of the corner of his eye, Vanye sees Lorn looking at him. He is surprised to see that the young lord looks at him, not with anger, but with some concern. "Do not harm him overly," Lorn warns the warriors.

(3) BURLY CHYA WARRIORS
*To hit Vanye: 12   To Be hit: 9   Hit points: 8*
*Damage with clubs:   Damage with longsword:*
*1 D6+1                2 D6*

# Section 51

> Damage with hands:
> 1 D6−2

*If Vanye is not in armor, his chance to be hit is 14.*

*There are three Chya Warriors. They fight to subdue. If Vanye goes below 1 hit point, he is unconscious.*

*If Vanye starts the fight weaponless, he can try to wrest a club from one of his enemies. To do this he must forego an attack. Roll 3 D6 against Vanye's Dexterity. If the roll is less than or equal to Vanye's Dexterity, he has the club, and will now do 1 D6+1 damage instead of 1 D6-2. If the roll fails, he is weaponless and has wasted an attack. He may make as many attempts to take the warrior's weapons as you wish.*

*If Vanye loses, turn to section 36.*

*If Vanye wins, turn to section 44.*

*If Vanye surrenders anytime during the fight, turn to section 81.*

# * 52 *

Vanye's heart pounds. These Leth warriors seek to deceive him. He does not know what foul designs they have on him, or why they are really leading him away, but he has no desire to know. His heart is pounding so hard he is sure the disguised men of Leth can hear it, but they say nothing. He wants to tell Lorn his warriors are spies from Leth. But then he has a sinking thought. It occurs to Vanye that Lorn may know of the warriors' deception. After all, he should know the histories and the families of all the men who rode with him.

And still they ride on. The hoofbeats of the warrior's horses ring in Vanye's ears. Each hoofbeat sounds like the ring of doom. Finally Vanye can not stand it any longer. Without warning he wheels his horse and bolts into the woods. The warriors stare after him. Lorn shouts, "Get him, you dolts!" The warriors grunt and spur after Vanye.

"Carefully! Carefully!" Lorn screeches, bouncing up and down on his mount as he chases after his warriors.

Vanye charges frantically through the woods, urging his weary horse on. His sudden flight has bought him some distance, but the warriors are riding hard behind him. He looks around for Chya patrols. He sees none. The disguised Leth warriors are gaining on his tired horse. They are not far behind him now.

Vanye suddenly veers sharply to one side, forcing one warrior off into the heavy undergrowth. The man swears as his horse stumbles in the bracken. The other two draw nearer.

Then Vanye spots Lorn, loping along well behind him, and to the right. Vanye realizes he has no chance of escaping the warriors, but he *could* distract them. He turns his horse sharply to the right, allowing the two remaining warriors to close on him. As they approach him he slows. They slow too. Then Vanye gives his horse a kick, and bursts past the warriors, riding straight for Lorn.

Lorn is reaching into his saddlebag. His face twists into a mask of fear and horror as Vanye bears down on him. He sits paralyzed for the instant before the two horses collide.

*Roll 3 D6 for Vanye's reckless charge. If the roll is less than or equal to Vanye's Dexterity, he has successfully ridden Lorn down. If the roll is greater than Vanye's dexterity, he has failed.*

*If Vanye fails, turn to section 48.*

*If Vanye succeeds, turn to section 72.*

# * **53** *

Vanye says, "Forgive me, but I do not wish to go."

Taomen stares in disbelief. "You . . . do not . . . *wish?*"

"Seek your business with my *liyo*, not with me," he says, feigning a confidence he did not feel.

Anger flashed across Taomen's face. "Impudent wretch of an *ilin!*" he snaps. "No one dismisses Chya Lorn's decree so uncaringly! You insult the honor of our hall!" In a single, clean motion, he draws his sword and charges.

*If Vanye should defend himself against the enraged Taomen, turn to section 46.*

*If Vanye should try to stop the impending fight by apologizing and agreeing to see Lorn, turn to section 60.*

*If Vanye should try to run away and find Morgaine, roll one free attack against Vanye by Taomen, and then turn to section 64.*

# \* **54** \*

Vanye says, "No, Chya Lorn. I cannot hide from her. You are a man of honor. You must understand. This is my final duty to her, to tell her I am out of her service. To do otherwise would be cowardice."

Angered, Lorn says, "Vanye, you cannot afford the luxury of such honor."

Quietly, Vanye replies, "If I cannot start my new life with honor, there can be no honor in it."

Lorn is perplexed. "Vanye, your honor will be the death of you."

"Perhaps," Vanye says. "But that is better than life without honor. You should understand that."

*Turn to section 51.*

# * 55 *

Vanye takes a deep breath, holds it a moment, and then says quietly, "She travels north to Hjemur, where she intends to kill Thiye and destroy the Witchfires there."

Lorn says nothing. Vanye feels edgy. He could well be oath-breaking. He is putting his trust in the honor of Chya Lorn. Lorn says nothing.

Finally, Vanye blurts out, "Now tell me, I pray you, how I may leave her. If you have not spoken truly about my being able to leave her service and regain my honor, my soul is . . ." He can not finish.

Lorn looks at him sympathetically, though somehow also coldly. "Fear not. I will tell you."

*Turn to section 69.*

# * **56** *

The more Vanye looks at Lorn, the less he can find troublesome. The man is perhaps less of a bold warrior than his station commands, but that is not an impossible occurrence. Vanye is sure there is nothing wrong with his newfound benefactor.

Vanye turns his attention to the other three men riding with them. The more he looks at them, the less they look like the tall, lean, quiet men of Chya. Rather, they have the rough, sullen look of the men of Leth.

And then Vanye realizes he has seen one of the men before, during the ride through Leth. The man was one of the Leth bandit-warriors. This knowledge strikes him like a sword blow. At least one of the warriors Lorn is trusting is an imposter, and not of Chya at all! Very likely all three are imposters. His life and Lorn's could be in great danger. He feels he should tell Lorn. Lorn is his new lord, and he owes Lorn allegiance. If he knows something Lorn does not, he is bound to tell him of it. But he will have to be careful, lest the men overhear him. Perhaps it would be better if he could attack the imposters by surprise . . .

# Section 56

His thoughts are racing so loudly, he is sure the other men can hear them. But they continue riding, apparently unconcerned.

Vanye feels very cold.

*If Vanye should just keep riding, turn to section 82.*

*If Vanye should keep riding but quietly tell Lorn that his men are really from Leth, turn to section 38.*

*If Vanye should turn and ride away in an attempt to escape them, turn to section 52.*

*If Vanye should attack the men, turn to section 47.*

# \* **57** \*

Vanye watches the fierce men of Leth surround him. He thinks of the ones he could take out with him; the weaker ones, the slower. He judges he can take four. Maybe five. And then he will be dead. He unhooks his weapons and lets them slip to the ground.

Lorn smiles a chilling smile. "Good of you to see this with such understanding," he says mockingly.

Vanye is quickly and securely bound and carried away. Soon he falls asleep from exhaustion and fatigue.

*Turn to section 31.*

# * 58 *

Vanye spots a door and bolts toward it. The bulky Leth warriors grunt and start after him, raising their net. They toss the heavy fishing net over him just as he reaches the door.

The warriors close in as Vanye struggles to dodge the net.

*Roll 3 D6 for the men throwing the net. If their roll is equal to or greater than 10, they have netted him, and Vanye must roll under his Dexterity to escape the net, during which turn he cannot attack. If the men can keep him netted for two consecutive turns, Vanye cannot escape and is captured.*

*If Vanye is captured, turn to section 77.*

*If Vanye avoids being netted for three consecutive turns, he escapes. Turn to section 74.*

# * **59** *

Vanye dodges aside at the last moment, causing Morgaine's sword stroke to whistle harmlessly past his ears. He scurries to his horse, keeping an eye on Morgaine. She looks at him with contempt, ready to take another swing. "If I see thee again," she says icily, "I will kill thee!"

She reins her horse around and thunders away northward. Vanye watches her go. His heart pounds, as if it is trying to burst. Slowly, as if in a daze, he mounts his horse. He lets the animal set a pace and choose a direction.

He can go anywhere. He is free of the witch at last. So why does he feel an ache in the emptiness that used to be his chest?

His eyes sting, tears blinding him. He rides south.

*Turn to section 29.*

# * **60** *

Taomen swings his sword at Vanye savagely. Vanye falls to his knees in submission, putting his hands up to protect his head. "Forgive me!" he pleads. "I did not understand. I will speak to Chya Lorn." He waits for the sword blow. It does not arrive.

Taomen grunts. "Well," he says. "That is atonement enough for your insolence, *ilin*. Come. Chya Lorn is waiting."

*Turn to section 41.*

# * **61** *

Vanye hesitates, then says, "Chya Lorn, if you command that I go with you and see your proof that Morgaine is *qujalin*, I shall do so. But until such time as I have such full proof, I am still *ilin* to her. My duty is clear. I must tell her I am going riding."

Lorn shakes his head, refusing to believe what he is hearing. "I do command you to go. And I forbid you to tell her."

"Chya Lorn, my first duty is to her. I must obey her first."

"I am truly sorry to hear that," Lorn replies. "It means I must exercise my power over you as lord in this house."

"You would take me by force?" Vanye asks incredulously.

"I suppose I have no choice," Lorn replies regretfully.

There is a moment of silence between the two.

*Turn to section 51.*

# \* **62** \*

Vanye watches the mounted men of Leth close in on him. He calmly draws his sword.

Lorn sees this, and says, "Now, Vanye, you are only wasting your time. Give up peacefully, and I will spare you unnecessary pain."

Vanye raises the blade.

"Now, Vanye, you really can't expect to win, you know. The odds are impossible!" Lorn cries.

Vanye stands his ground.

"All right, then," Lorn says viciously. "Get him, you dolts, but don't damage him. I've no wish to suffer pain from your carelessness."

The Leth warriors advance.

Shouting so loud it startles the warriors, Vanye cries out, "Hai, my ancestors! Hai, my Chya mother! I come to join you!"

Lorn screams in anguish and terror.

*Turn to section 29.*

# * **63** *

Vanye says, "I am *ilin*. You must ask my lady her business."

Lorn looks at Vanye understandingly. "Vanye, the woman you serve is as inhuman as the Witchfires themselves. She deceived the ten thousand who followed her one hundred years ago, and she deceives you. It is her way."

"The ten thousand could have followed her out of loyalty. No one knows for certain . . ."

"She heads north, does she not?"

"It is her business. Ask her."

"What would she want in the north? There is nothing there but Hjemur and great evil. What does she want?"

"Again, inquire with her as to her business. Not her servant."

"Hmm. You are a stubborn one, Nhi Vanye. And yet you are a man of honor. You favor your Chya heritage in that. I like that. Because you are honorable, I will tell you a secret. Are you interested? I can tell you how you may honorably be free of service to the sorceress, and also regain your lost honor. I know how you may be a full man again."

*Turn to section 69.*

# * **64** *

Vanye's heart is pounding. He must get away to warn Morgaine of the treachery in the house. He runs from the gathering warriors, toward the stairs, shoving men aside as he goes. He is out of his armor, and can move faster than men encumbered with heavy armor.

They catch him as he reaches the stairs. One warrior grabs his arm, and another his hair. They drag him to the ground. He tries to call Morgaine, but a kick to the ribs robs him of his air.

He tries to protect himself from the rain of blows that fall on him from the enraged warriors, but it is useless. As his vision begins to fade .to gray, he sees his brothers, and relives their cruelty and torment.

*Roll against Vanye's Constitution on 3 D6. If the roll is less than Vanye's Constitution, he has survived the beating. Turn to section 31.*

*If the roll is greater than Vanye's constitution, he has died under the savage attack. Turn to section 29.*

# * **65** *

Vanye considers the scribe's words: "Do you mean . . . you will pay me to flee Morgaine's service?"

The old man nods. Vanye's honor rankles at the thought, but he bites down on his pride, and bows his head. "Take me from here," he says softly.

"Gladly," says the scribe, and the light in his eyes does not seem quite so dull.

The scribe claps his mottled, dry hands, and four Leth warriors enter the stable. "Warriors, take this worthy gentleman to a safe place, where the sorceress cannot find him." To Vanye he says, "We will deal with the witch ourselves. Never you fear."

The warriors prepare a wagon, and tell Vanye to climb on. Vanye replies that he prefers to ride his horse, but they are adamant. They do tie Vanye's horse to the back of the wagon.

One of the warriors cracks a whip, and the team of horses pulls the wagon out into the night air. The warriors laugh and swear heartily enough, but they seem nervous.

Once they are out of sight of Lord Grivvis' hall, one of the men of Leth on the wagon

## Section 65

strikes Vanye a cruel blow with a club. The blow is not enough to rob Vanye of his senses, but it does stagger him, he turns to defend himself, and the driver of the wagon strikes him. Vanye falls under the onslaught. The Leth warriors laugh heartily, bind him, and turn the wagon toward Lake Domen.

*Turn to section 79.*

# * **66** *

Vanye stands stock still. He watches his *liyo* stoically as her sword bites deeply into his armor and sinks into his shoulder. White hot pain flashes through him, and he falls to his knees.

"Excuse my disobeying an order," he says. "I only know my duty." The world sways, and grows distant to him.

Morgaine drops off her horse. She catches his swaying body, and cradles it in her arms.

"Forgive me," she says.

Vanye nods. He knows a lord never has to ask forgiveness of an *ilin*. Not for any affront. But she has done so, and he gives his forgiveness willingly, for he understands.

In that moment, arriving from the direction of Lake Domen, he could have been anyone in Vanye's body. He could especially have been Lorn.

Morgaine has too much at stake to risk riding with a *qujal* enemy. She has to be sure. Better by far to fail her *ilin* than to fail her mission. So she put him to a test that only the true Vanye could pass.

He understands, but it makes him shiver to

## Section 66

think of the sort of creature to which he has given oath.

At length she binds his wound, and helps him back into his saddle. He feels weary, but contented.

"Come," she says. "We will quit this place, and find our way to Hjemur, where Thiye's head shall be ours."

Vanye smiles, and follows her into the growing light of dawn.

*The Adventure is concluded. Vanye and Morgaine ride from here into Hjemur and destroy the Gate there, and through it all Gates on this world. And when Morgaine passes through the portal before its destruction, Vanye follows.*

# * 67 *

Vanye bows, and says, "I will go." He rises to follow with Taomen. Then he stops. He feels somewhat afraid to enter the presence of the younger Chya lord. If Lorn would ignore custom by conducting the master's business with the servant, there is no telling how many other courtesies he would disregard, including breaking codes of peaceful conduct.

Vanye's eyes fall on his armor on the floor by the hearth. He would be more comfortable in his mail. If there is treachery, it might help him survive long enough to alert Morgaine.

But then, requesting to don his armor could be viewed as an insult, suggesting that he did not trust his host. Vanye was torn. Another moment and Taomen will lead him away from the hearth, and the decision will be made for him.

*If Vanye should ask to stop to quickly don his armor, and risk insulting Chya Lorn, turn to section 70.*

*If Vanye should leave his armor by the hearth and go to speak with Chya Lorn, turn to section 41.*

# * **68** *

Vanye tries to grasp Changeling. The unfamiliar-ly lean muscles in Lorn's body move spastically under his command, but he is able to clutch the sword, and draw it. It vibrates with lunatic power, sending a shock through him, and making his hand and arm ache. An unholy inky opalescent field pours forth from the area where the blade should be. At the sight of it, Lorn, in Vanye's body, suddenly looks afraid.

The sword pulses with great and savage power. Vanye directs the shimmering black field at the area between the standing stones. There is a roaring sound, as if the gods themselves are wailing. Lorn in Vanye's body shrieks as the backlash tears him apart. He is whipped into the darkness and disappears.

Vanye feels the vibrations grow more and more intense, until the backlash rips him apart as well. Then there is oblivion.

*Turn to section 29.*

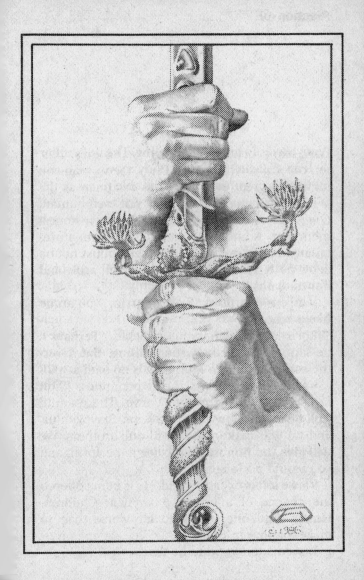

## * **69** *

Lorn leans forward, and narrows his eyes. "Listen carefully, Nhi Vanye i Chya, the woman you serve is a great evil. She is as inhuman as the Witchfires themselves. A thing not even human. *Qujal*. Vows are only binding between honest men and women. An oath to an unnatural creature need not be kept. Indeed, must not be kept, as it makes a mockery of all true and honest oaths."

Vanye is confused. "For a warrior, you argue like a scholar."

Lorn laughs, a nervous chuckle. "Perhaps," he says, "I am in the wrong calling. But nevertheless, your oath to Morgaine is no oath at all."

Vanye is speechless. Lorn continues, "You favor your Chya heritage, Vanye. There could well be a place for you in Ra-koris. Stay with us, and we will make you one of our brothers. We will give you honorable service to perform, and you would no longer be *ilin*."

Vanye looks up, surprised. He is being offered the chance of a home. A woman. Children. Honor. And one could do far worse than to make a home in Ra-koris.

It seems too good to be true.

"And of course, you would be a warrior again," the young lord adds, offhandedly.

Vanye feels dizzy with disbelief over his good fortune. "Do you speak truly?"

"My honor on it. We will tell her you are out of her debt and in our care. She can scarce keep a claim on your soul when you are no longer *ilin*. And if she does dare start a fight over her false Claiming of you, our warriors would be marshalled against her. We are willing to do that for you. So, she would not risk fighting us all. Let her follow her sorcerous path. You will have a home."

Vanye cannot speak for a moment.

*If Vanye should accept the offer, turn to section 45.*

*If Vanye should reject the offer, turn to section 34.*

## * **70** *

Vanye dashes back to the hearthside and grabs his armor. If there is treachery afoot, he will have a better chance of surviving it armored. It is worth risking the potential insult to Chya Lorn.

Taomen turns, puzzled and impatient. Vanye says, "I am not presentable in these travel-worn clothes." He quickly pulls on his armor. Taomen scowls.

It pains Vanye to wear the heavy mail while his skin is still chafed from wearing it for too long. Having it off even briefly has been a blessed relief.

Vanye straps his weapons on as well. Taomen begins to speak, but seems to think better of it, and does not. He leads the armored Vanye into a small room, where Chya Lorn sits alone. Lorn dismisses Taomen.

Chya Lorn welcomes Vanye warmly. If he is insulted at Vanye's being armored, he does not voice his displeasure.

*Turn to section 41.*

# * **71** *

Vanye rides through the Koris woods like a man possessed. Strange creatures skitter past his horse in the dim starlight. Huge serpentine abominations slither about his horse, frightening the beast, and Vanye has to struggle to maintain control. Cruel, bestial eyes glint in the dark, and unnatural noises drift up from hollow logs and waft down from drooping tree branches. Vanye thunders on, unheeding.

He rides toward new Ra-koris, searching for Morgaine, and dreading finding her. The *qujalin* blade that he recovered weighs heavily on him. It frightens him. And she frightens him even more.

Vanye savagely reins his panting horse to an abrupt standstill. He freezes, straining to listen past the noises of the night. He hears the sound again; the sound of a galloping horse. No matter who it is on the roads, Chya or Leth, it does not bode well for him. He tries to hide his horse, but still the hoofbeats grow louder. He turns to go the other way, but the rider plunges out of the bracken and crosses his path.

It is Morgaine.

Vanye stares, disbelieving.

## Section 71

"*Liyo*," he says. "I must tell you what happened . . ."

She cuts him off with a brusque motion of her gloved hand. "Changeling. Has thee it?"

Vanye grabs Changeling from among his saddle bags. "I have recovered your blade, Lady. Take it quickly. It frightens me, and I do not covet it."

"Indeed," says Morgaine coldly. She takes Changeling, and straps it in its place. Then she turns to leave. Vanye follows. She looks at him coldly. "What does thee desire now, *ilin*?" she snaps.

Vanye opens his mouth to speak, but cannot.

"There is nothing thee can do for me," she says. "Thy return of Changeling allows thee to sever our bond, as we agreed."

Vanye feels unsure of himself. "We agreed . . . ?" he asks.

"Aye. Your oath, that should Changeling be lost to me and thee recover it, your bond be broken. Go. You are *ilin* to me no longer." She turns to ride toward the far north horizon.

"Lady. *Liyo*! We had no such agreement! Please, I am no sorcerer, and do not understand tricks and games of the mind. But however you seek to confuse me, I know we had no such agreement. Unless you give me an honest reason why my obligation is discharged, I am still bound to you!" Vanye feels sick as he pleads. It would be the ruin of his soul to be forced to break his oath without reason.

"I have told you my reason. Leave my side or I will slay thee." She draws her secondary sword, and holds it above him. Her eyes are as serious as the grave. He hesitates.

And she swings the sword downward.

*If Vanye should accept Morgaine's orders and leave, turn to section 59.*

*If Vanye should stay and be cut down, turn to section 66.*

# * **72** *

By the time Lorn realizes what is happening, Vanye is upon him. Vanye's horse crashes into Lorn's with a sickening thud. Lorn flies from his horse and hits the ground hard. Vanye manages to hold on, and stay in the saddle.

In the instant before the collision, Lorn had been frantically rummaging through his copious saddlebags, searching for something. When the horses collided, Lorn's equipment, including Changeling, went flying.

Changeling, still in its sheath, clatters to a stop near Vanye's horse's hooves. Vanye stares at the hated weapon for a heartbeat. Without thinking, he scoops it up, and rides away into the underbrush.

Behind him he can hear the warriors stop their horses. He also hears Lorn gasp for breath and plaintively wail, "Don't help me, you louts! You're wasting time helping me! Him! Get him!"

But when the hoofbeats start up again they are far behind him.

*Turn to section 71.*

# * **73** *

Vanye feels himself sinking deeper into Lorn's body. He watches his own face leer down at him. It is the most frightening thing he has ever seen. He wants to flee from it, to escape the shock of it forever; to sink into the dark where sorcerers cannot menace him.

Then blessed oblivion takes him and he feels no more.

*Turn to section 29.*

# * **74** *

Vanye runs through the halls of the mansion, oblivious to pursuit. His heavy footsteps kick up dust, and rats scurry away at his approach. Ugly children pop their heads out of doors like vermin, and laugh at him. Vanye dashes past the gloom-filled, vacant rooms, and heads toward the noise and light of people. Morgaine has to be somewhere in this house of madmen.

He hears her voice somewhere in the distance, and feels a surge of elation. He is surprised to find that he considers her a safe refuge. Her. Morgaine.

She says, "What do I receive for this *qujalin* knowledge?"

A man's voice answers, "If you will tell us how to finish our work with the Gates, we will offer you a full kingdom within the new empire of Leth, which will encompass all this land from . . ."

Vanye rounds the final corner, and bursts into a smokey room where several of the men of Leth sit around a scarred table. Morgaine sits among them, a soft, white-robed figure of elegance among men of coarse, matted fur and armor.

Morgaine turns to Vanye, upset at the interruption. Some of the men laugh. "What's this?" says one. "Can you teach your servants no better manners than to race through good men's halls?" All the others laugh, their oily faces twisting into mockeries of smiles. Vanye looks behind himself nervously.

Morgaine's voice carries over the noise. "What is it, Vanye?" she says calmly.

"Forgive me, lady. They tried to take me from you against my will."

"Speak," she says, and a hush falls on the chamber. Vanye quickly explains to her what has happened. When he is finished, Morgaine looks the man at the head of the table squarely in the eye. "So this is your hospitality, Lord Grivvis?"

Lord Grivvis seems disturbed, but dismisses the episode with a wince and a wave of his hand. "Forget the *ilin*, he is unimportant. What is important . . ."

"No, Lord Grivvis," she replies icily. "It is very important. How you treat my servant reflects how you will treat me." She rises from her chair and walks to Vanye. She places one hand on his shoulder, and leans against him, as if to comfort him. Vanye flinches from the shocking and unexpected familiarity of her touch. He is appalled by what he was told she is, and yet oddly drawn to what he knows she is. His musings are interrupted, as she sharply hisses, "Saddle the horses," in a tight whisper. She

## Section 74

wheels and faces the men of Leth. Vanye turns from her and slips away.

"Lord Grivvis," she says. "You have broken custom with me. I can no longer accept your hospitality."

A great furor rises in the hall. Leth warriors stand to stop her. She glares at them, and some shrink from her gaze. But some do not.

Vanye hears sounds of arguing coming from the great hall, and then the delicate sound of blades sliding from scabbards. He considers returning to fight beside her, but he has a duty. And yet, what sort of duty would he have if she is killed?

*If Vanye should return to Morgaine and fight at her side, turn to section 27.*

*If Vanye should continue to the stables, turn to section 76.*

# * **75** *

Vanye tries to grasp Changeling. The lean muscles in Lorn's body move spastically under his command, but he is able to clutch the sword, and draw it. It vibrates with lunatic power, making his hand and arm ache. An inky opalescent field pours forth from it. Lorn in Vanye's body looks afraid.

Vanye feels a great ache. He wishes to atone for his deeds by his own hand. Far better to die, even at the hand of sorcery, than to have his body stolen for another's use.

So he lowers the field onto himself, Lorn's body.

He sees Lorn, in Vanye's body, scream in rage. He feels himself ripped up from the ground and hurled into cold pain. Then there is nothing.

And then, inexplicably, he feels the transference process reverse, snapping him back into his own body. He sees Changeling on the ground, field still roaring as the men of Leth disappear into it. It howls as if it is trying to suck in the world.

Vanye snatches the weapon up, and sheaths it. The chaos stops.

## Section 75

The hill is gutted and barren. And deathly still. Vanye aches. But the air tastes sweet, and he is struck by the power of the realization that he is alive.

He carefully wraps Changeling up, and walks down the hill to where the men had left their horses. He selects one, and rides north, seeking Morgaine, unsure of how he can find her, but sure that he will.

*Turn to section 71.*

# * **76** *

Vanye hears sounds of battle behind him and winces. Morgaine could die because he refused to turn back. But he keeps running. He has been told his duty, and he will obey it to his last breath. He reaches the stables, and is relieved to see that no one is there.

Frantically, he saddles the horses, Morgaine's first. As he is saddling his own, he hears an unearthly roaring moving down the hall toward him. He hears groans of terror, fear and great pain. None sound like Morgaine.

She bursts into the stables, sheathing her sword, Changeling. Grimly she leaps onto her horse, and rides out without a word. Vanye finishes saddling his own mount and follows after her.

They have ridden for some time before he dares ask her of the fight. He asks how it is she survived. She replies, "Changeling is a powerful weapon. Like the Gates themselves, it opens a gulf to an elsewhen that is hungry for all things. None can stand before it."

"Not even armies?" Vanye says, almost accusingly.

"I did not kill the ten thousand," she replies.

## Section 76

"Thiye did. With the Gate at Hjemur. I go to avenge those men, and see to it such things can never happen again."

"How?"

"The void that is unleashed when Changeling is drawn is sufficient to destroy a Gate. And its user. But remember, Vanye, you have sworn to destroy the Gate if I cannot."

"I will hold to my oath," Vanye answers.

*Turn to section 35.*

## * **77** *

The Leth warriors grunt triumphantly as they net the wriggling, swearing Vanye. They wrench his sword from his hand, and carry him out of the stable in an undignified, but strangely gentle manner. There they dump him unceremoniously into a wagon.

The wagon rolls away from the crumbling stone hall, and down along the blighted lands of Leth, toward Lake Domen.

*Turn to section 79.*

# * **78** *

Vanye tries to grasp Changeling. The lean muscles in Lorn's body move spastically under his command, but he is able to clutch the sword and draw it. It vibrates with lunatic power, making his hand and arm ache. An inky opalescent field pours forth from it. Lorn, in Vanye's body, looks afraid.

Vanye lowers the field onto Lorn, and watches as his body is swept into the void. He hears his body scream. Then he feels the transference process losing its grasp on him, and he feels his mind hurtling into the void, transferring back to its original body. Then he feels darkness, and peace.

*Turn to section 29.*

# * **79** *

The wagon takes Vanye to a field of standing stones near Lake Domen. He is dragged up a bare hill, to where a Gate stands. The Gate is much like the Gate Morgaine had come through when he first saw her.

The scribe hobbles up the hill, and looks Vanye over. "Yes," he says. "I shall enjoy this body."

Vanye's throat is hoarse and dry. "Why . . . ?" he croaks.

"If Morgaine thinks I am you, she will tell me her secrets. Besides, I am long past due for a new body. Cheer up, young one. You will soon rule the world!" He laughs a long, obscene laugh.

The shimmer of the starfield in the Gate pulses and hums. Vanye feels a sinking sensation, and then void.

*Turn to section 29.*

# * **80** *

The more Vanye looks at Lorn, the more comfortable he feels. The man is perhaps less of a bold warrior than his station commands, but that is not an impossible occurrence.

Vanye turns his attention to the other three men riding with them. The more he looks at them, the less they look like the tall, lean, quiet men of the Chya. Instead, they have the rough, sullen look of the men of Leth.

And then Vanye realizes he had seen one of the men before, during the ride through Leth. The man is one of the Leth bandit-warriors. This knowledge strikes him like a sword blow. At least one of the warriors Lorn is trusting is an imposter, and not Chya at all! Very likely all three are imposters. His life and Lorn's could be in great danger. Unless Lorn knows who and what they are . . .

Vanye's thoughts are so strong he is sure the other men should be able to hear them. But the warriors continue riding, unconcerned.

And Vanye suddenly feels very cold.

*If Vanye should just keep riding, turn to section 43.*

*If Vanye should keep riding but quietly tell Lorn that his men are really from Leth, turn to section 38.*

*If Vanye should turn and ride away in an attempt to escape them, turn to section 52.*

*If Vanye should attack the men, turn to section 47.*

*If Vanye should attack Lorn, turn to section 84.*

# * **81** *

The night air is particularly fragrant outside new Ra-koris. The ride takes Vanye, Lorn and the three burly Chya warriors through rustic meadows and valleys. Lorn speaks pleasantly, and the warriors hold their tongues. But Vanye is not enjoying the ride. He feels uncomfortable about being commanded to leave Morgaine. Lorn's genial manner now does not change the fact that Vanye was taken against his will.

And yet, what if Lorn spoke the truth? If Morgaine is indeed an inhuman beast, to enter into an agreement with her would be frightfully wrong. Lorn would then be helping Vanye's imperiled soul by ending his contract with Morgaine. All the legends said she was an inhuman, *qujalin* creature.

The longer he thinks about it, the worse he feels. Vanye morosely berates himself for being foolish enough to enter into a contract with her. And yet, he had found peace, of sorts, serving her and riding with her. He had not considered this until now; until he was suddenly faced with the prospect of losing his *ilin* status. He enjoys her company. He is strangely drawn to her tan, white-maned elegance . . .

Vanye abruptly stops his thoughts there. He refuses to allow himself to harbor such thoughts about something that should seem a creature as inhuman as the Koris Wolf he had faced earlier. It must be that some artifice, some *qujalin* sorcery was used to blind his reason and attract him so. But how could even sorcery affect him so completely, on so many different levels?

There is too much to consider. His thoughts are whirling and spinning and getting nowhere. He resolves to stop brooding about Morgaine. He will wait till he has proof. He will decide his course of action then. Any speculation before then would be futile. And yet, what if she turns out to be an inhuman monster? What then? He would have to leave her service . . .

Vanye decides to occupy his mind with something else before his head splits apart from worry. Vanye realizes that Lorn has been speaking to him all during his reverie, so he decides to begin paying attention. Lorn is chatting amiably about the recent victories of the Chya people. Vanye listens to the young lord for a few moments, but finds his mind straying again and again to the problem of Morgaine.

To keep his mind off Morgaine, Vanye begins to study the things around him intently. He scrutinizes the trail they are following, the condition of the Chya horses, the rough faces of the warriors . . .

And then something begins to bother Vanye. Something feels out of place. Vanye dismisses

## Section 81

the feeling. No doubt it is fatigue, or some nagging concern over having left Morgaine without her knowledge. He winces at the thought, and puts it out of his mind.

But something keeps buzzing around in the back of his mind. He peers at Lorn, looking for clues, but he can see nothing wrong with the young lord.

*(Note—if Vanye did not have his weapons and armor in the preceding encounters, Lorn graciously allowed him to get them before the ride. For future encounters, Vanye is armored.)*

*Roll 3 D6. If the roll is less than or equal to Vanye's Wisdom plus two, he has succeeded in figuring out what is bothering him. If the roll is greater than his Wisdom plus two, he has not worked it out.*

*If Vanye makes the roll (rolls less than his Wisdom plus two), turn to section 80.*

*If Vanye fails the roll (rolls more than his Wisdom plus two), turn to section 43.*

## \* **82** \*

Small, unformed doubts skitter around in Vanye's mind, as in a murky pool. They won't leave, but they also won't come to the surface. Finally Vanye puts the whole worry behind him. It is likely no more than his fear of Morgaine. To dispel these thoughts, he concentrates on what Lorn is saying. Lorn is still cheerfully discussing Vanye's new life with the Chya.

"You will enjoy our hunts. You seem a skilled warrior, and I'm sure you will be a valuable addition to our ranks."

Vanye takes a deep breath, and starts to relax. His doubts fade like morning mist.

Though the journey is very pleasant, Vanye soon begins to feel disoriented, as if he isn't sure where they are going. At length he says, "Lorn, how much further is it?"

Lorn smiles a cold smile and says, "We shall be there in a moment. I am as eager to be there as you." Vanye feels vaguely disconcerted by this, but there is no problem he can identify. So he continues on.

Soon he sees the single jagged tower of old Ra-koris jutting above the tree line. It is said to be the only portion of the old keep still standing. The rest had been razed, and now is in ruins.

## Section 82

Lorn looks more excited than Vanye, and squirms happily in his saddle. Lorn leads the men into a clearing. Now Vanye can clearly see the ancient ruin of Ra-koris. Huge stone blocks and columns lie strewn about the place, and burnt timbers scrape against the sky like an immense, broken ribcage. One tower still stands, defiantly cutting into the sky. The remains of the other towers are barely discernible amidst the rubble. A twenty foot wall rings the whole camp, though it is breached in places.

Lorn pauses a moment, studying the place. "The shortest route to your estate passes through here," he says. "Have you ever been in the old Ra-koris keep?" he asks cheerfully.

Vanye shakes his head slowly. He is not sure he wants to enter, but he says nothing.

Lorn smiles, motions with his hand, and leads the way into old Ra-koris through a crumbled part of the wall. The warriors silently follow him. Vanye looks into the silent woods, and rides after them.

As he crosses the threshold, Vanye shudders. The ruins have a forbidding air, and he feels as if his presence there is somehow defiling the sleep of the ancient stones. Still, it was made by men's hands, and was not a foul *qujalin* ruin.

Deep shadows fill most of the ruins, and the ground is treacherous. Several times Vanye's horse loses its footing. Then the beast shies. Vanye reins to a halt to find what is troubling it. From deep in the ruins he hears another horse whinny and stamp. He quickly reins around to ride the other way, but a dozen men of Leth on horseback begin to close in from behind Vanye and Lorn. Twenty more emerge from the gloom in front of them. Vanye looks to Lorn for help. For Leth to harm Lorn would invite serious Chya reprisals. And at the least, Lorn's ransom would be far greater than his own.

Lorn backs away from him, saying to the men of Leth, "Please take him gently. I do not wish to feel undue pain when I take his body."

Vanye feels his heart leap into his mouth. He knows all is lost, and he curses himself for falling into such a trap. He has almost no chance fighting against so large a group, and he can see no avenue of escape. If he surrenders, he might live. But then, would he not be better dead than suffering whatever foul *qujalin* rites Lorn has planned?

In his mad panic, he hears his father's voice, commanding him to fall on his own blade, to die an honorable death for killing Kandrys. He could not do it then, and so he was doomed to a life as an honorless *ilin*. Could he do it now?

The men close on him slowly.

*If Vanye should fight, turn to section 50.*

*If Vanye should surrender, turn to section 57.*

*If Vanye should try to flee, turn to section 85.*

*If Vanye should kill himself, turn to section 62.*

# * **83** *

The roaring black void descends toward Vanye, stars twinkling within it. Trees and leaves and sticks rush into its hungry maw. Vanye gapes at it in abject fear. The *qujalin* sorcery before him will surely destroy his soul. How could he even receive an honest burial if his body is pulled into the awful blackness of the sword along with the whirlwind of leaves and sticks?

"Lorn! You will kill your men!" Vanye shouts over the deafening roar. He is almost pleading. Lorn smiles a twisted leer, and continues lowering the starfield.

Vanye struggles for a moment with the men he is fighting, and then stops resisting. "I surrender. I surrender, damn your eyes!"

Lorn smiles wider. The field descends slightly further. Vanye feels a chill pass over him, as if all the warmth around him were being leeched into the hungry void beyond the sword. Lorn lets the feeling last a moment.

Then, slowly, Lorn raises the sword. The black field moves with it. Lorn lifts the sheath above the blade, and brings it down over the weapon, as if he is scooping in the howling darkness.

The roaring quiets and the swirling black field

## Section 83

disappears within the confines of the scabbard. Lorn smiles, quite pleased with himself.

The Leth warriors lose no time in grabbing Vanye and tying him with a stout length of cord. Vanye feels weak, and sways giddily, overwhelmed by the experience.

The warriors drag Vanye back to his horse. "Carefully, you dogs!" Lorn warns. For any pain he feels I will repay you in kind one thousand-fold." The warriors gingerly raise Vanye to his horse. Vanye looks at them in disgust.

Methodically, Vanye begins looking for an escape. It will be a long ride to the Witchfires, if that is indeed their goal. Lorn seems to sense his thoughts.

"I want him unconscious," Lorn commands imperiously. The warriors look at one another uneasily. None step forward.

"You!" Lorn says, pointing to the shortest of the three. "Render him unconscious, but do not hurt him."

The warrior unslung his club and cautiously steps up to Vanye, who leans away to avoid the blow. The other two men hold Vanye still, while the one with the club strikes. Pain floods across Vanye's head, but the blow was too light, and Vanye remains agonizingly conscious.

"Fool!" Lorn rages. Vanye braces himself, and the warrior strikes again. This time the pain is followed by darkness and blessed release.

*Turn to section 31.*

# * **84** *

The burly Leth men bob up and down on their horses, oblivious to Vanye's penetrating stare. He knows they were imposters, but does Lorn know?

Lorn continues chattering happily. If he knows the men are Leth, he betrays no sign of it. But he has to know. He should know the men who serve him; know their families and histories. One in Lorn's position would hardly entrust himself into the hands of men he was not familiar with.

He did know. He had to know.

Vanye scowls at Lorn. Lorn is a traitor. A traitor to Vanye, to the Chya, and especially to Morgaine.

He must go back. He must escape. He will have trouble against three men, but Lorn . . .

Vanye rides over to Lorn's horse, suddenly quite fascinated by the young Lord's words.

Lorn smiles, glad to see Vanye taking an interest in what he has to say. Vanye smiles back. Then Vanye leans over to Lorn, as if to murmur some trifling confidence, grabs Lorn about the neck and cruelly tightens his grip.

Lorn sputters, choking.

## Section 84

The disguised Leth warriors turn and stare at Vanye incredulously. Vanye slides his knife from his belt and presses the blade tightly against Lorn's throat.

The Leth warriors utter oaths and kick their horses into a desperate pace to close on Vanye.

"Back!" Vanye shouts. "Or your master dies!"

The men clumsily turn their horses aside, and ease them back.

When they have moved far enough away to satisfy Vanye, he speaks to Lorn. "You will answer all my questions or your neck will grow a second mouth," he says hoarsely. Then he slowly, cautiously, loosens his stranglehold on the Chya lord.

"Why do you use Leth warriors? No lies!" Vanye demands.

Lorn wheezes for a moment, gasping for breath. But he says nothing.

"Speak!" Vanye commands, bristling with the mounting tension.

"They are much more reliable than those Chya fools," Lorn replies at last. "Their loyalties are easily bought. They don't waste a lot of thought on honor."

"Are you betraying the house of Chya?"

"Of course. And many others, besides."

Vanye shifts uncomfortably in his saddle, unprepared for such candor. He has greatly underestimated the Chya lord's capacity for evil.

"What do you want of me?" Vanye asks.

"Morgaine's secrets, of course."

Vanye laughs out loud; the tension draining out of him over the absurdity of it all. Lorn looks faintly annoyed.

"Then you are a fool, Lorn," Vanye says, releasing his grip somewhat. "I know little more than anyone."

"Ah, but you could learn much in your time with her."

"I would never tell one such as you her secrets."

"You wouldn't have to. I would see them first-hand."

Vanye stares at Lorn blankly.

"Vanye, Chya Lorn has been dead for weeks," Lorn says.

And Vanye understands. He feels a sinking feeling in his stomach, and his legs go weak. Lorn hits Vanye in the ribs, and the dagger flies from Vanye's hand. Lorn quickly reaches into his saddlebags.

*Roll 3 D6 against Vanye's Strength.*

*If the roll is less than or equal to Vanye's Strength, Vanye has not lost his grip. Turn to section 87.*

*If the roll is greater than Vanye's Strength, turn to section 90.*

# * **85** *

Without a word, Vanye kicks his horse's flanks, and dashes around the ruins looking for a breach in the ring of the thirty-odd Leth warriors closing in on him.

He sees none. The gaps between the horsemen are small and growing smaller as the Leth riders approach.

Vanye spots a gap between two riders that is slightly larger than the others. He desperately wheels his horse and rides toward it. The Leth riders smile, ugly, gap-toothed grins as he approaches them. One raises a club, and the other brandishes a net. The looks on their faces and their enthusiasm show that they take great pleasure from such sport.

Quickly, Vanye turns his horse before he reaches them. There would be no way past them. He scrambles to evade them, and sees that the warriors behind him have closed ranks. There is no way out.

His horse nearly stumbles on a jutting rock, then refuses to move. Its hoof is trapped, stuck, wedged in a break in some rotting boards. Keeping one eye on the circling Leth warriors, Vanye coaxes the horse to pull its foot straight out of the hole. The horse's leg comes free, shattering some of the rotting boards.

As the hoof comes out of the hole, Vanye catches a glimpse of something on the ground, but a sudden burst of hoofbeats from behind him causes him to gallop away before he can study it further. He barely manages to dodge a net thrown by the approaching rider.

The ring of Leth warriors is practically upon him. Vanye can see Lorn's twisted smile in the half-light.

*Roll 3 D6 against Vanye's Wisdom. If the roll is less than or equal to Vanye's Wisdom, he has identified what he spotted on the ground. If the roll is greater than his Wisdom, he has not identified the object.*

*If Vanye has identified the object, turn to section 89.*

*If Vanye has not identified the object, turn to section 91.*

## * **86** *

The narrow slits of the wolf's eyes burn into Vanye's skull. The beast stares, unmoving and unblinking, cold eyes full of death. Vanye stares back, trying to mimic the hate in the wolf's eyes, and trying to keep his fear from showing through.

The quiet night noises become deafening to Vanye as the contest of wills rages. Sweat wells up under Vanye's headband, threatening to pour into his eyes and blind him, but he does not wipe it away. His back begins to ache, but he holds his position. Then his leg begins to grow numb. He knows that if he's not concentrating when the wolf leaps, he will not be able to move quickly enough. So he stares on, determined not to move.

Suddenly the wolf's eyes blink. Then fear enters the wolf's red eyes, and Vanye can taste victory. He growls gutturally to frighten the beast.

The wolf turns and flees, howling furiously. The cry of the wolf chills him to the marrow. It sounds almost like a man. With the Koris Wolf gone, Vanye relaxes. A wave of relief washes over him. He has saved his wounded *liyo*, Morgaine, and the thought makes him feel even better. He stirs the fire enthusiastically.

Then he sees that Morgaine is watching him.

"Trouble, *ilin*?" she asks.

"Nothing," he replies modestly. "A Koris Wolf. I drove it off. It must have feared the fire. Did its howling wake you?"

She nods. "They have an unsettling wail."

Vanye thinks about the wolf, and its eyes, so intelligent, and so cruel. The thought makes him shudder. He stares into the fire. All he can see is the eyes of the wolf, boring a hole into his soul.

"Is something troubling thee, *ilin*?" Morgaine asks.

Had she read his mind? Were his mind and soul an open book to her? No, it could not be. Vanye refuses to accept that. She is merely wise in the ways of people.

He slowly nods. "The beast. The Koris Wolf. How does Thiye make such things?"

"He does not so much make them as draw them through," she replies. "He uses the Gates to reach places where such things are normal, and brings them here, where they are not natural. Many die. But some live and breed. They are driving away all native life here. If Thiye is not stopped, soon all the world will be as the Koris woods are now."

Vanye shudders. His thrill of victory is gone now, and he feels cold.

## Section 86

*If Vanye is wounded, turn to section 9.*

*If Vanye is not wounded, turn to section 22.*

# * 87 *

The blow to his ribs did not hurt Vanye, but serves to snap his attention sharply back to where he is and what he is doing. Lorn does not seem to have a warrior's strength. If there is indeed a *qujalin* sorcerer in Lorn's body, it is likely he was not a skilled fighter. The thought is not a great comfort to Vanye, but it does raise his hopes.

Lorn was fumbling frantically among his saddlebags. He pulls out a sheathed sword. Vanye grabs Lorn's arm and wrenches it. Lorn cries out in pain, and drops the weapon, which clatters to the ground. It is Changeling.

The sight of it paralyzes Vanye for an instant, but then catapults him to action. He strikes Lorn in the stomach and pushes him from his horse. The lord strikes his head on the ground, and moans weakly.

Acting almost without thought, Vanye leans down low, almost falling out of his saddle, and makes a grab for Changeling. He snatches the weapon by the cool metal sheath and spurs his horse off into the woods, toward new Ra-koris.

He glances over his shoulder, and sees that the three Leth warriors are not chasing him.

## Section 87

Instead they are huddled over Lorn, checking to make sure he is all right.

Vanye chuckles to himself. That's what comes of hiring mercenaries, he thinks. If their employer dies, they lose all interest and go home. Far in the distance he faintly hears Lorn wail, "After him, you fools! He escapes!"

But soon the sounds of their hoofbeats have died out behind Vanye.

*Turn to section 71.*

* **88** *

The narrow slits of the wolf's eyes burn into Vanye's skull. The beast stares, unmoving and unblinking, cold eyes full of death. Vanye stares back, trying to mimic the hate in the wolf's eyes, and trying to keep his fear from showing through.

The quiet night noises become deafening to Vanye as the contest of wills rage. Sweat wells up under his headband, threatening to pour into his eyes and blind him. He does not wipe it away. His back begins to ache, but he holds his position. Then his leg begins to grow numb. He knows that if the wolf leaps while he is unprepared, he will not be able to move quickly enough to avoid it. He begins to grow afraid. The wolf's nose pushes forward slightly. Vanye stiffens. Has the wolf sensed his doubt? Vanye grows worried. He fights to keep his concentration, but the cruel light in the Koris Wolf's eyes cuts into him. Finally he can not take it any longer.

He closes his eyes and looks away for a moment. In that instant the wolf leaps. It crashes into Vanye, its great bulk pushing him back

## Section 88

several feet. They crash out of the clearing and roll into the woods.

With a heave, Vanye pushes away from the great Wolf, and fumbles for his weapons.

*Roll 3 D6 against Vanye's Dexterity. If the roll is less than or equal to Vanye's Dexterity, Vanye has gotten out his sword. While Vanye is fumbling for his sword, the Koris Wolf gets a free attack. If the roll is greater than Vanye's Dexterity, Vanye has failed to draw his sword. Vanye may try to get his sword in every round, but forfeits his attack every round he tries. If he opts to fight with his dagger, he does not have to roll or lose an attack to draw the weapon.*

KORIS WOLF
*To hit Vanye: 12   To be hit: 9   Hit Points: 8
Damage with claws   Damage with
and fangs: 1 D6+1   longsword: 2D6
                    Damage with dagger: 1 D6*

*The Koris Wolf attacks with a ruthless savagery. It will fight until it kills or is killed.*

*If Vanye is killed, turn to section 29.*

*If Vanye kills the Koris Wolf, turn to section 17.*

# * **89** *

The Leth warriors close in like a clamp. Vanye knows there is no way to break through their human wall. He will go down before them like a sapling in a gale. Lorn knows that. It is why he has chosen to bring thirty to subdue one.

Vanye feels a strange surge of pride that Lorn felt he needed so many to take one bastard *ilin*.

Vanye checks his horse to see if it had injured its foreleg freeing its hoof from the hole.

He has no wish for the horse to be injured in the melee. The noble beast should not have to suffer for the idiocies of men. He is relieved to see there is no sign of a wound.

As he rides, Vanye studies the way the horse has come, to make sure it will not step through the rotting boards again. Then his eye catches the outcropping he had seen before.

It is barely more than a broken ring of stone around a hole partially covered with rotting boards, but it was once a well. Vanye has a wild thought to leap into the well, swim through the underground streams below and escape to freedom. His chances would be negligible. and he knows it.

## Section 89

*If Vanye should leap into the ancient well shaft, roll 3 D6 against his Constitution. If the roll is less than or equal to Vanye's Constitution, turn to section 95.*

*If he leaps and the roll is greater than Vanye's Constitution, turn to section 98.*

*If Vanye should instead fight the Leth Warriors, turn to section 50.*

*If Vanye should surrender to the Leth Warriors to avoid a fight, turn to section 57.*

*If Vanye should kill himself, turn to section 62.*

* **90** *

Vanye doubles over from the force of Lorn's blow. His side feels like it is on fire. Lorn quickly backs his horse away from Vanye. Vanye forces himself to straighten up, and face Lorn. He takes a reckless swing at the man, but Lorn has moved out of reach. Vanye's fist barely grazes the young lord.

Lorn pulls his hand from his saddlebag. He is gripping a sheathed Changeling. Vanye stops short in fear. A wicked smile twists across Lorn's face as he slowly slides the blade free.

In horror, Vanye stumbles backwards. As the gleaming sheath slips from the blade, the woods are filled with a horrible roaring sound. An inky, opalescent field whirls violently from the blade of the unsheathed weapon. The air is rent with unearthly screams as leaves, branches and uprooted trees hurtle through the air, plunging into the void that gushes from the sword.

Transfixed, Vanye stares at the unnatural sight before him. Lorn holds the sword straight up, and sweeps the trees above him into the void, where they vanish. As Vanye gapes, the disguised men of Leth creep up behind him. Two grapple with Vanye, and throw him from his horse. They roll on the ground, kicking and gouging.

"Surrender, Vanye, or die in agony," Lorn cries, as he watches Vanye's fear with obvious relish. Vanye struggles wildly, but the two men hold him firmly. The foul *qujalin* void that spills forth from Changeling would destroy him as surely as it destroyed the forest around them. But if he surrenders he might meet a far worse fate.

Would the sorcerer-lord kill his own Leth warriors in order to get Vanye? A look at the madness etched on Lorn's face answered that question. Lorn is revelling in the destruction he is causing. He leers with lunatic glee as he lowers the sword's field toward Vanye.

*If Vanye should surrender, turn to section 83.*

*If Vanye should continue fighting, turn to section 92.*

# * **91** *

As Vanye watches, the Leth warriors close in like a clamp. Vanye knows there is no way to break through their human wall. He will go down before them like a sapling in a gale. Lorn knows that. It is why he had chosen to use thirty warriors to subdue one.

Vanye feels a strange surge of pride: that Lorn felt he needed so many to take one bastard *ilin*.

Vanye checks his horse to make sure it had not injured itself when its hoof was lodged in the hole. He is glad to see the horse is fine. In the approaching melee, he does not want the horse injured. The noble beast should not have to suffer for the idiocies of men.

His eye traces the way the horse has come, to make sure it will not step through the rotting boards again. But he can not spot the place in the dim starlight. He will have to ride back blind and hope for the best.

"Give up, Vanye! It won't do you any good," Lorn cries out. The Leth warriors are now so close Vanye can smell their soiled armor and fetid breath. Vanye turns his horse and crashes into one warrior, trying to burst past him. The Leth warrior jerks his reins backwards in surprise, and nearly falls from his horse. Another warrior takes a swing at Vanye with a club. The warrior is fighting to subdue, and the blow bounces ineffectually off Vanye's armor.

In a frenzy, Vanye thinks he sees an opening, and rides toward it. Two warriors are upon him in that instant. One threw a net on him, and the other strikes him with a club. Vanye spurs his horse on, and is yanked from the saddle by the net. He tumbles to the ground, and his horse gallops on. One Leth warrior still holds the end of the net securely.

Vanye tries to stand, but the warrior viciously yanks the net, and sends Vanye sprawling to the rocky ground. The more Vanye struggles, the tighter the net winds about him.

As he attempts to rise, a club blow cracks along the side of his head. Sparks fly before his eyes, and the sight of the ugly warriors about him grows hazy. Then black.

*Turn to section 31.*

# * **92** *

"Unholy beast," Vanye shouts over the roar of the void that spills from Changeling. "I'll not give in to the likes of you! I'll see you dead first!" He strikes at one of the men of Leth who is holding him down. The warrior groans in pain and rolls away. The other warrior kicks at Vanye, but keeps an uneasy eye on Lorn.

Lorn just smiles enigmatically.

The ferocious roar that issues from the sword grows more intense, as it nears Vanye and the warriors. One man still holds Vanye.

"Fool!" Vanye shouts at the man. "He means to kill us both. Release me."

Fear steals over the warrior's face as the inky cloud approaches them. Stars twinkle within the opalescent field. The Leth warrior freezes, paralyzed by the approaching void. Vanye can feel a strong wind blow up, pulling leaves and debris past them and toward the blackness. The chill of it spurs him to action.

Summoning his strength, he pushes the warrior from him, turns and runs. He hears a horrid shriek behind him, and the sound of the warrior's voice fades, as if it is coming from a

## Section 92

great distance. It has not yet died out completely when the field envelops Vanye.

At first Vanye feels the cold. The cold of the field is greater than any he has known, even in the cruelest winters. The ground beneath him rushes away from him with a wrenching heave. He tumbles dizzily around, as the air gushes from his lungs, and stars spin about him.

Frenziedly he looks down, and sees Lorn's twisted smile. Then the blackness takes him, and silence descends.

*Turn to section 29.*

* **93** *

With a jolt, Vanye finds himself falling into a deep pit. He scrapes his hands against the dry walls of the well to slow his fall. In the dark his shoulder strikes something solid, and his desperate fingers reach out for it. He misses it, and continues falling. Without warning, he hits a grate at the bottom of the dry well. The impact stuns him.

As he lies weakly at the base of the well, he hears echoing voices float down from above, angry and frightened. "There! Down in the well!"

Vanye groans. The voices from above grow indistinct, and the little circle of light far above him sways.

"If he's dead you will all pay dearly," a scratchy voice says; probably Lorn's.

Then there is a bright flash from above, and a brightly burning torch drops down the shaft toward Vanye, illuminating the shaft as it goes, and spraying sparks and embers when it hits the walls. Vanye weakly moves his hands to cover and protect his eyes.

The torch hits the grate at the bottom of the shaft, a foot from Vanye, and fizzles weakly.

## Section 93

"There he is!" a deep voice shouts.

Vanye looks around, and sees that there is no way out but up. The iron grate below him prevents further escape. He tries to stand, but he knows it is useless.

"You," he hears Lorn's fading voice shout. "Get a rope and climb down. And he had better be unhurt!" There is a scrambling noise, and a few rocks fall in the well shaft, clattering on Vanye and the grate.

He waits for the Leth warriors to arrive, but his pain grows great, and he collapses in exhaustion.

*Turn to section 31.*

# * **94** *

In a frenzied moment, Vanye has a wild idea to pull Changeling from its sheath and unleash its foul *qujalin* magicks. He is in Lorn's body, so the blade is at his hip. He could draw it and try to use it for revenge.

But he comes to his senses. He realizes that drawing the accursed weapon would imperil his soul. Better to face the evil you know than the evil you don't.

Vanye feels a great weakness come over him, and he sinks in a heap. He sees his own face looming over him. It is Lorn, smiling cruelly. Then blessed darkness takes him from the world.

*Turn to section 29.*

# * **95** *

"Give up, Vanye! It won't do you any good," Lorn cries out. The Leth warriors are now so close Vanye can smell their soiled clothing and fetid breath. Vanye turns his horse and crashes past one warrior, heading back to the well. The Leth warrior jerks back on his reins in surprise, and nearly falls from his horse. As Vanye passes a second warrior, the warrior swings a club at him. The warrior is fighting to subdue, and the blow bounces ineffectually off of Vanye's armor. Vanye rides through a hail of clubs that rises and falls, rises and falls on his body. Despite the pain, Vanye continues on.

Vanye approaches the well, but several Leth horses prevent his horse from maneuvering nearer. He sees another warrior ready for a cudgel blow. Vanye slips from his saddle to the ground and the warrior strikes Vanye's horse. Vanye feels a strong sense of regret at the horse receiving a wound in his place.

The men of Leth laughed obscenely as Vanye slips from his horse. "Here are the tactics of the Nhi!" says one. "He thinks he will fight better from the ground."

"He wishes to beg mercy on bended knee!"

another adds. Vanye maneuvers between the horses, running for the well. The warriors are too busy laughing to stop him. They know he can not get past them. As Vanye leaps toward the well he hears Lorn cry, "Look out, fools, he is up to something!"

Vanye crashes through the rotting boards covering the well, and plummets into the blackness below.

*Roll 3 D6 against Vanye's Dexterity. If the roll is less than or equal to Vanye's Dexterity, turn to section 101.*

*If the roll is greater than Vanye's Dexterity, turn to section 93.*

# * **96** *

Vanye leaps toward the two bored Leth warriors. Their eyes flash open, and a look of shock and bewilderment hangs on their faces. It is as if they have seen sorcery: a man fell down a well, disappeared, and emerged from the earth covered with blood and dirt.

They are sluggish in bracing for a fight, Vanye sees and he exploits a few good openings before they even have their swords in hand.

They begin shrieking for help, and the other Leth warriors near them run to their aid.

(2) LETH WARRIORS
*To Hit Vanye: 13   To be hit: 9   Hit points: 5*
*Damage with clubs:   Damage with longsword:*
*1 D6+1                    2 D6*
*                               Damage with dagger:*
*                               1 D6*

*The men of Leth fight to subdue. If Vanye drops to 1 hit Point, he is unconscious.*

*Vanye gets one free attack before the men can fight back. Since Vanye attacks first in the combat round, he will get two attacks before the Leth Warriors get one. New warriors will arrive to* take up the fight on the fifth round of combat. If Vanye has not killed the two warriors by the third round a new Leth warrior will join the fight on the fourth round. Another will show up on the fifth round, the sixth round, and so on, until the tenth round or Vanye is captured, or escapes. (There are a total of thirty-five Leth Warriors in Old Ra-koris but no more than ten can fight Vanye at one time.) Vanye may flee the fight at any time, but when he does, all warriors engaged in the fight, including those waiting their chance, will get one final swing before he gets away.

If Vanye kills the two men before the others attack him. turn to section 107.

If Vanye is killed, turn to section 29.

# * **97** *

Summoning his courage, Vanye approaches the slumbering creature. It looks deceptively peaceful in its sleep. He hopes with all his heart it will stay that way. He silently pads across the bone-strewn chamber, carefully avoiding the debris.

He reaches the sleeping body of the creature. Up close, the creature's stench is overwhelming. Vanye pauses to listen to it breathing. The creature's rasping breath is still deep and regular. Assured the creature sleeps on, Vanye cautiously steps past it. In a flash the creature grabs Vanye's leg in a viselike grip, and sends him crashing to the ground.

Vanye cries out in fear. The creature had been pretending to be asleep. It had probably smelled Vanye as soon as he was in the cavern. Vanye curses himself for having been taken so easily. He knew the creature was intelligent. He should have suspected that it was capable of some sort of ruse.

He fumbles for his sword, and sees the creature's other huge fist sweep past him.

PIT MONSTER
*To Hit Vanye: 10   To be hit: 12   Hit points: 20*

Damage with claws:
2 D6+2

Damage with longsword:
2 D6

Damage with dagger:
1 D6

*The Pit Monster is cunning and strong, but not too fast. It will try to hold on to Vanye so Vanye cannot escape before it has mauled him to death. If Vanye should try to dislodge the creature's grip on his leg, roll 3 D6 against Vanye's Strength. If the roll is less than or equal to Vanye's Strength, Vanye has freed his leg. If the roll is greater than Vanye's Strength, he is held firmly. Vanye cannot attack in the same round he is trying to get his leg free.*

*If Vanye kills the Pit Monster, turn to section 100.*

*If Vanye is killed by the Pit Monster, turn to section 29.*

*If Vanye should break loose and flee during the fight, the creature gets one last attack while Vanye runs. Turn to section 103. (Note that Vanye cannot flee while his foot is held.)*

# * **98** *

Vanye feels a consuming frenzy to reach the well. Leaping into an abandoned well could be a fatal mistake, but in the heat of the frustrating battle, it seems like his only choice.

Lorn cries, "Give up, Vanye! It won't do you any good." The Leth warriors are now so close to Vanye that he can smell their soiled clothes and fetid breath. Vanye turns his horse and crashes past one warrior, heading back to the well. The Leth warrior jerks back on his reins in surprise, and nearly falls from his horse. As Vanye passes a second warrior, the man swings a club at him. The warrior is fighting to subdue him, and the blow bounces ineffectively off Vanye's armor. Vanye rides through a torrent of cudgel blows. The pain is severe, and the world begins to slip from his sight.

Vanye approaches the well, but several Leth horses prevent him from maneuvering his horse nearer. Through a haze he sees another warrior raise a cudgel. Vanye slips from his horse to the ground and the warrior strikes Vanye's horse. Vanye's legs buckle as he hits the ground, but he manages to prop himself up on the horse as the horse snorts in pain. Vanye feels a strong sense of regret at the horse receiving a wound in his place, but he pushes on.

The men of Leth laugh obscenely as Vanye staggers among the rubble. "Here are the tactics of the Nhi!" says one. "He thinks he will fight better from the ground."

"He wishes to beg mercy on bended knee!" another adds. Vanye maneuvers between horses, loping toward the well. The warriors laugh as Vanye tries to push past them. They know he can not get past them.

Lorn shouts, "Get him, fools! He is undoubtedly up to something!"

Vanye sees the well a mere six feet away. The ground is spinning uneasily beneath his feet, and the well before him slowly bobs up and down. He staggers toward it, his hands over his head to fend off blows. One Leth warrior kicks him in the stomach, and another hits him on the head. Vanye crashes in a heap.

*Turn to section 31.*

# * **99** *

Scarcely breathing, Vanye studies the slumbering creature. It looks deceptively peaceful in its sleep. He hopes with all his heart it will stay that way.

The passage beyond the creature beckons, tantalizing; just out of reach. But the risk is too great. Vanye decides to wait. Hopefully the Leth warriors will soon give up looking for him and leave. Then he can climb out the well without disturbing the great creature.

He silently pads out of the bone-strewn chamber, carefully avoiding the debris. The creature sleeps on, a broad grin on its wide mouth.

Warily, Vanye sits down just beyond the bend in the passage. That way he can keep an eye on the beast, and notice it if it stirs. Vanye relaxes, listening to the creature breathe. Its rasping breath is deep and regular; almost soothing.

Then one of its huge eyes opens, and pops shut again. Vanye is paralyzed with terror. Did it merely twitch in its sleep? Or is the monster only pretending to sleep? Motionless, Vanye keeps watching.

The creature opens a bleary eye again, and

©1981

## Section 99

glances around the chamber. Vanye does not dare to move.

A frown crosses the beast's huge face. The scent of its prey is further off now and it is upset. The creature begins sniffing the air, its animal snout flaring. But it does not move or make a sound. If Vanye had not chosen to keep an eye on it, he would not even know it was awake.

He thinks about turning to flee, but he is afraid doing so would attract the creature's attention.

Then he hears footsteps behind him. Lorn's men have discovered his escape tunnel. By waiting, he has lost the little lead he had gained. The creature suddenly notices the noise, and closes its open eye, pretending to sleep. It waits for more prey to stumble on its lair.

*If Vanye should run away down the corridor toward Lorn's men, turn to section 102.*

*If Vanye should attack the beast, turn to section 110.*

*If Vanye should wait where he is, turn to section 108.*

# * **100** *

The huge beast gives with one torturous cry, and falls to the ground with a crash, splintering the bones that litter the floor, and sending brittle fragments flying. Vanye slumps against the cavern wall, gasping for breath.

The fight is over. He has killed the beast. He can scarcely believe it, but he *has* killed it. It fought with inhuman strength and cunning, but had died like any mortal creature. It now lies at Vanye's feet, blood pouring from its many wounds, spilling into its matted, shaggy hair and welling out on the floor in puddles.

When Vanye regains his strength, he takes a burning piece of wood from the fire and staggers on down the cavern. The glowing brand does not give the light of a torch, but it is better than nothing. For a moment Vanye fears it may reveal his presence to his foes. What if the caverns are full of those things?

He puts such thoughts out of his head, and continues on. He finds he can move faster now. With the light from smoldering wood he can see the ground before him, and does not have to grope blindly.

He walks for what seems like a long time before the passage slopes upwards again. Cau-

## Section 100

tiously, Vanye creeps forward. The passage becomes so steep he is forced to climb. He carefully places his brand on the ground. If this is not an exit he will need it again.

The going is slow, as Vanye makes his way up the dark slope. He skins his hands on the sharp rocks, but his armor protects the rest of him.

Soon he smells fresh air, and hears voices from above. He pulls himself up and listens. Two greasy Leth warriors are talking. "He's gotten clean away in those tunnels," says one.

"Ahh," grunts the other. "He hasn't a prayer. Lorn's sorcery will flush him out like a rat before long."

"We best hope so," the other agrees.

Vanye pushes away the debris in front of him. Cool air rushes in, feeling exquisite on his flushed and sweaty face. He looks through the hole and sees the two warriors. The rest of the men of Leth are off in the distance. They have a bonfire going near the well Vanye had leapt into.

Just past the two men are some horses. There are a few scruffy Leth-bred horses, and one sleek black Chya mount. The black is obviously Lorn's.

Vanye hauls himself from the dirt and prepares to run.

*If Vanye should attack the two Leth warriors, turn to section 96.*

*If Vanye should try to avoid the warriors and run toward the horses, turn to section 105.*

# * **101** *

Tumbling in air, Vanye finds himself falling into a deep pit. He scrapes his hands against the dry walls of the well to slow his fall. In the dark his shoulder strikes something solid, and his desperate fingers reach out for it. His grasp holds the thing, and his wild plummet stops with a sharp jolt. It is an iron bar imbedded in the well wall. It twists and buckles in his grasp, but it holds. His arm feels like it is on fire, and he can hear the bones in his shoulder creak. Echoing voices float down from above, angry and frightened.

He hauls himself up to the bar, and tries to lean against the well wall for support. The wall is broken and jagged in places. Vanye leans against it, momentarily loses his balance, and falls backward.

For a frenzied second, Vanye thinks he is falling deeper into the well, but he hits solid flooring. He realizes he is in a small tunnel leading from the well shaft.

The voices from above grow more insistent. "There! Down there!" a deep voice shouts. "If he's dead you will all pay dearly," a scratchy voice says, probably Lorn's.

## Section 101

A torch falls past Vanye, illuminating the shaft as it goes, and spraying sparks and embers where it hits the walls. Vanye crouches deeper into the tunnel to avoid the light. The torch hits the grate at the bottom of the shaft, and fizzles weakly.

"Er . . . he's not in there," a guttural voice says. Vanye decides not to wait any longer. He crawls down the dark tunnel on his hands and knees. The tunnel is almost wide enough for him to walk, but crawling is quieter, and gives him the option of holding on if the tunnel suddenly drops away.

"You," he hears Lorn's fading voice shout. "Get a rope and climb down. And don't come back without him. Unhurt!" There was a scrambling noise, and a few rocks fell in the well shaft, clattering on the grate below.

The tunnel Vanye is in slopes down, and becomes wider. Soon the sounds behind him fade away. He is in some sort of underground tunnel. It was a passage possibly cut into the rock so the Chya could secretly flee the city in times of siege, Vanye thinks hopefully. If he is right, he can use it to flee to safety.

But it is more likely to be some sort of overflow channel for the well. He will likely run into water or obstructing rock.

Vanye's musings are interrupted by an odd rumbling sound ahead. Vanye's heart jumps. In a moment of fear he thinks it is a rock slide, but the sounds are too rhythmic for that. He approaches cautiously, and smells something like cooked meat mixed with a sour, rancid odor.

It is something alive. Something huge is breathing deeply; snoring in the dark. Vanye rises to his feet, and approaches cautiously, acutely aware of every scrape of his boots on the stone beneath him.

He rounds a bend in the cavern, and sees a dull reddish glow. Thick, oily smoke fills the chamber. In the soft light, Vanye sees the floor of the chamber is strewn with bones. Many are deer and small game bones, but among them are human skulls. There are also skulls Vanye cannot identify.

The rasping, rumbling noise is louder now, and coming from the far corner of the cavern. Crouching behind the bend in the cavern wall, Vanye peers at the area the sound is coming from. He can barely make out a huge, furry lump, like a small hut covered in animal hides. Then he sees the head.

It is a monstrous shaggy man-creature. Its ponderous head is two feet wide, and its chest is almost four feet across. It has short, stumpy arms and legs, and a huge maw reaches from one side of its misshapen head to the other.

Vanye shudders. He has no interest in fighting such an unnatural beast. It is undoubtedly another of the creatures the sorcerer Thiye has drawn through the Gates. But unlike the Koris Wolf, this creature uses fire. It could be a cunning opponent.

# Section 101

In the dim firelight, Vanye can see that the passage continues beyond this one chamber. The beast's body is blocking the way.

*If Vanye should try to sneak past the hideous creature, roll 3 D6 against Vanye's Dexterity. If the roll is less than or equal to Vanye's Dexterity, turn to section 97.*

*If Vanye should try to sneak past the creature and the Dexterity roll is greater than Vanye's Dexterity, turn to section 104.*

*If Vanye should attack the creature, turn to section 106.*

*If Vanye should go back and take his chances fighting Lorn's men, turn to section 109.*

*If Vanye should wait in the cavern for Lorn and his men to go away, turn to section 99.*

* **102** *

A deep sense of dread wells up in Vanye. He feels surrounded; trapped. Frightening as the men of Leth are, with their cruel faces and overwhelming numbers, they are still human. The monster of the caverns is not of the natural world. His sojourn into the pits has served to plunge him only deeper into anguish. He longs for the strife and weariness to end.

Vanye chooses the doom he knows over the doom he doesn't. He races down the hall toward the Leth warriors; charging into the fight as if he is greeting old comrades.

The twelve men of Leth in the dark passage are so startled at Vanye's sudden reappearance that they aren't able to stop him before he has charged well into their ranks.

After a brief scuffle, the Leth warriors manage to subdue Vanye; netting him and clubbing him into unconsciousness. One remarks on how odd it is that Vanye seemed so eager to get out of the caves. Then they hear the creature.

Only four of the twelve Leth warriors who entered the cavern get out, but they do manage to get the unconscious Vanye out with them.

*Turn to section 31.*

# * **103** *

A faint gasp escaping from his lips, Vanye turns and flees the slavering creature. It howls in disgust, and lumbers after him, kicking bone fragments from its former guests aside as it goes.

Vanye feels hot and flushed as he runs. There is not much air in the passage, and running hard is an ordeal. His armor chafes against him and the straps constrict him, restraining him from running at full speed.

He cannot see his way in the rocky passage. He prays he remembers it well. He scrapes his head along the low part of the passage, and is surprised at how fast he has come upon it. He is nearly at the well opening.

He listens behind him. With luck, the beast has given up on its faster prey. But echoing stamps soon prove otherwise. Vanye takes to his feet again, running hunched over along the low corridor to the well.

Ahead he sees light pouring in from the opening in the passage. He can see the wall of the well across from the opening. Distorted voices float from above and below. "There's no way he could have opened it!" from below, and

"Keep looking! He didn't just vanish!" from above.

Vanye breathes a sigh of relief. They have not discovered the hole he had crawled into. He looks behind and hears the pit monster's labored breathing getting closer. He looks ahead and sees ropes dangling into the pit.

It is now or never. He has no choice.

He leaps out into the well shaft, grabs the rope, and hauls himself up, pulling with all his strength. One of the Leth warriors at the bottom of the well looks up and says, "Hey . . ." in helplessness and disbelief.

He is out of the well in a flash, and has knocked over two of the Leth warriors before the warriors notice him in the light of the bonfire that blazes near the well. "It's him!" one shouts. Vanye kicks him over before he can pull out a weapon.

Leaping jagged rocks, Vanye runs across the field. A circle of six warriors in front of him closes on him, cutting off his escape. He pauses for a moment, bracing for the final conflict.

And then he sees a look of horror flash across their faces. They stare past him in mute terror. Vanye stands perplexed. Then he hears the screams behind him. He turns around slowly and sees the pit monster wading through the Leth ranks, swinging the body of a Leth warrior, and scattering men like broken dolls.

The slavering creature meets Vanye's eye, and Vanye is sure the beast will charge after him.

But the monster snorts and turns away, wading into the thickest ranks of Lorn's men. It has given up on its former prey in favor of a banquet, and it has let Vanye know that. It will let him go in return for being led to so much food.

Gratefully, Vanye moves on. The six warriors that had confronted him have routed, some running to slay the beast that was killing their kin, some running to flee the carnage, and some just running.

Lorn's voice rises above the din. "Get out of the way, fools!" There is a bright flash of white light followed by a searing noise, and one of the men of Leth falls dead. Lorn swears.

The Leth warriors are scattered. Vanye walks over to the area where they had tethered their horses. Several of the Leth run by him without stopping—seeking escape.

After studying the remaining scruffy Leth horses briefly, Vanye selects the magnificent black Chya-bred mount that Lorn had ridden. He swings up into the saddle, and turns to leave.

As Vanye is easing the horse over the rubble, the area is faintly lit by another of Lorn's searing blasts. There is a pause, and then a massive crash. The Leth Warriors shout in triumph.

Again Lorn's reedy voice sails above the confusion. "Where's Vanye? Who's got him?" Silence. Vanye quickens the horse's pace. "Did you toads let him go?" Lorn thunders. "I'll have all your souls!"

## Section 103

"There he is, Lord Lorn," one mumbling voice replies. "There, on your horse."

Lorn's cry split the air, growing fainter behind Vanye. "No, no nooo!" Lorn wails. "You idiots! He's got Changeling!"

Vanye's ear barely catches the last word, and he turns around in the saddle, incredulous. He doesn't have . . .

Hurriedly Vanye rummages among the saddlebags. He pulls out the sheathed Changeling, gleaming in the star light. He is filled with awe and fear. Hurriedly he spurs his horse back toward new Ra-koris.

*Turn to section 71.*

# \* **104** \*

Summoning his courage, Vanye approaches the slumbering creature. It looks deceptively peaceful in its sleep. He hopes with all his heart it will stay that way. He silently pads across the bone-strewn chamber, trying hard to avoid the debris. His foot barely brushes a stack of bones, and the whole pile topples over with a splintering crash that echoes through the chamber. Vanye feels a flash of fear wash over him, paralyzing him.

But the creature sleeps on. Incredulous, Vanye takes a tentative step forward. He hesitates, and listens. The creature appears completely oblivious to the noise. Vanye creeps forward, studying the broad grin on the creature's wide mouth.

He reaches the sleeping body of the creature. Up close, its stench is overwhelming. Vanye pauses to listen to it breathe. The creature's rasping breath is still deep and regular. And then it occurs to Vanye that the creature might just be pretending to sleep, to lure Vanye into its grasp. The thought chills Vanye. Apart from the strange smile on the monster's face, it betrays no expression.

Vanye steps back. If the beast is waiting for

him to take one step closer, it might show some sign of concentration. Vanye backs into more bones, and sends them skittering across the floor.

He studies the beast from a distance. One eye opens and glares at Vanye.

With a roar of anger at having been out-smarted, the creature leaps to its feet. It snarls, dripping saliva from its massive jaws, and barrels toward Vanye in a slow, lumbering charge.

PIT MONSTER
*To Hit Vanye: 11   To be hit: 10   Hit points 20*
*Damage with claws:   Damage with longsword:*
*2 D6+2                2 D6*
                      *Damage with dagger:*
                      *1 D6*

*The Pit Monster is cunning and strong, but not fast. In addition to doing damage, its first hit will cause the monster to hold Vanye and keep him from escaping. If it succeeds and Vanye should try to dislodge the creature's grip on his leg, roll 3 D6 against Vanye's Strength. If the roll is less than or equal to Vanye's Strength, Vanye has freed his leg. If the roll is greater than Vanye's Strength, he is held firmly. Vanye cannot attack in the same round he is trying to free his leg.*

*If Vanye kills the Pit Monster, turn to section 100.*

*If Vanye is killed by the Pit Monster, turn to section 29.*

*If Vanye is able and decides to flee, turn to section
103. If Vanye flees after making at least one
attack, the creature gets one last attack while
Vanye runs. (Note that Vanye cannot flee while
his foot is held.)*

# * **105** *

Quietly, Vanye pulls himself from the hole in the ground. A cloud of dust swirls around him. He bursts into a run, and breezes past the two bored Leth warriors. Their dull, glassy eyes flash open, and a look of shock and bewilderment crosses their faces as they see a man, covered in dirt and blood, dart past them. When they realize it is Vanye, they sluggishly stomp after him, bellowing and coughing and calling to their fellows.

Other Leth warriors nearby hear them, and run after the first two. Vanye glances over his shoulder and sees the lumbering mob by the flickering light of the bonfire.

Turning from the approaching horde of warriors, Vanye vaults a fallen column and runs for the Leth horses. He reaches the clearing where the horses are tethered, studying the mounts as he runs. He tries to choose among the collection of mangy, scruffy Leth horses, looking for a capable one.

Then his gaze falls on the sleek black charger that Lorn rode in on. Vanye's eyes glow with a special fire. The beast is magnificent. It has strength and character. It is obviously Chya-

bred. To leave it in the hands of Leth, or worse—
*sorcerers*, seems a great waste.

Quickly Vanye unties the beast, puts his foot
in the stirrup, and strikes the horse's flank. The
black bursts into motion, and Vanye swings
himself into the saddle as the horse runs.

He charges toward the nearest group of Leth
warriors; scattering them and keeping them
from their mounts at the same time. The Leth
are not entirely cowardly, and are soon able to
order their ranks for another attempt at the
horses. When they regroup to charge him,
Vanye turns and rides the other way, guiding the
sure-footed beast over the debris and toward the
far wall. If he can reach it before the Leth have
mounted and given chase, he is sure he can lose
them in the forest beyond.

Behind him Lorn's voice wails plaintively,
"Don't let him go! Oh, by the Void, don't let him
go!" Vanye smiles grimly. Defying sorcerers
pleases him.

Soon he reaches the breach in the great wall
surrounding Old Ra-koris. Behind him are only
a few warriors, their clumsy mounts laboring to
find a clear path through the rubble. Vanye
laughs to himself and sends the black flying into
the night, toward new Ra-koris, and Morgaine.

*Turn to Section 71.*

# * **106** *

Silently, skillfully, Vanye draws his longsword. He knows he has but one chance to kill the beast. If his first stroke does not suffice, he could perish. He cautiously approaches the slumbering creature. It looks deceptively peaceful as it snores. He hopes with all his heart it will stay asleep.

Carefully measuring each step, he silently pads across the bone-strewn chamber, trying hard to avoid the debris. His foot gently brushes some bones, and they make a faint clattering noise as they fall. He hesitates, and listens. The creature appears completely oblivious to the disturbance. Vanye creeps forward, and tensely studies the broad grin on the creature's wide mouth, searching for some sign of awareness.

But it seems the creature sleeps on, completely indifferent to the intruder. Vanye takes another tentative step forward.

He reaches the sleeping body of the creature. Up close, its stench is overwhelming. Vanye pauses to listen to it breathe. The creature's rasping breath is still deep and regular. Vanye raises his sword and aims a blow.

He loses his balance and topples over backwards, a huge hand gripping his leg. The beast has moved like lightning, and grabs Vanye before he can strike with the sword. Vanye is struck with amazement even as his body crashes to the cavern floor, scattering dry bones.

It suddenly occurs to Vanye that the creature was only pretending to sleep to lure Vanye into its grasp. It had probably smelled Vanye since he first entered the cavern. But Vanye has no more time for thought.

The creature is on its feet, looming above Vanye, still clutching his leg. It snarls, and drips saliva from its massive jaws. Vanye desperately tries to fight it off, though he is lying almost helpless on the ground.

## PIT MONSTER

*To Hit Vanye: 10(8)   To be hit: 12(14)   Hit points: 20*

| | |
|---|---|
| *Damage with claws:* | *Damage with longsword:* |
| *2 D6+2* | *2 D6* |
| | *Damage with dagger:* |
| | *1 D6* |

*The Pit Monster is cunning and strong, but not fast. It will try to hold onto Vanye's leg to keep him from standing up. While Vanye is on his back, the Pit Monster has to roll 8 or better to hit Vanye, and Vanye has to roll 14 or better to hit the Pit Monster. The only way Vanye can stand is to pull his foot free from the monster's grasp.*

*If Vanye should try to dislodge the creature's grip on his leg, roll 3 D6 against Vanye's Strength. If*

# Section 106

the roll is less than or equal to Vanye's Strength, Vanye has freed his leg. If the roll is greater than Vanye's Strength, he is held firmly. Vanye cannot attack in the same round he is trying to get his leg free.

If Vanye kills the Pit Monster, turn to section 100.

If Vanye is killed by the Pit Monster, turn to section 29.

If Vanye is able and decides to flee, turn to section 103. The creature gets one last attack while Vanye runs. (Note that Vanye cannot flee while his foot is held.)

# * **107** *

Blood spatters against broken ground and sinks into the thirsty dust as Vanye plows through the Leth warriors before him. More are on the move, running toward him in the flickering light of the bonfire.

As he turns from the approaching hoard of warriors, Vanye vaults a fallen column and runs for the Leth horses. He reaches the clearing where the horses were tethered, studying the mounts as he runs. He tries to choose between the collection of mangy, scruffy Leth horses, looking for a capable animal.

Then his gaze falls on the sleek black charger that Lorn had ridden. Vanye's eyes glow with a special fire. The beast is magnificent. It has strength and character. It is obviously Chya-bred. For it to end up in the hands of Leth, or worse, sorcerers, seems a great waste.

Quickly Vanye unties the beast, puts his foot in the stirrup, and strikes the horse's flank. The black bursts into motion, and Vanye swings himself into the saddle as the horse runs.

He charges toward the nearest group of Leth warriors, scattering them, and keeping them from their mounts at the same time. The Leth

# Section 107

are not entirely cowardly, and are soon able to order their ranks for another attempt at the horses. When they have regrouped enough to charge him again, Vanye turns and rides the other way, guiding the sure-footed beast over the debris and toward the far wall. If he can reach it before the Leth have mounted and given chase, he is sure he can lose them in the forest beyond.

Behind him Lorn's voice wails plaintively, "Don't let him go! Oh, by the Void, don't let him go!" Vanye smiles grimly. Defying sorcerers pleases him.

Soon he reaches the breach in the great wall surrounding Old Ra-koris. Behind him are only a few Leth warriors, their clumsy mounts still laboring to find a clear path through the rubble. Vanye laughs to himself and sends the black flying into the night, toward new Ra-koris, and Morgaine.

*Turn to section 71.*

# * **108** *

With mounting dread, Vanye listens to the clatter of Leth footsteps behind him, and the rasping, regular breathing of the creature before him. He knows he can go no further either way. He is trapped between the hammer and the anvil.

Pain wells in his chest, and he thinks of his life. Warriors always behind him, and the strange world of *qujalin* magic before him, misty and unknown. He always feels off guard, always out of balance in his life—the footsteps grow louder. The creature's breathing grows more intense—and yet, lately, he has been content. Almost happy. How? It occurs to him that recently he has been squarely straddling his life and fate. He has not been dragged about by the caprices of fate like some peasant, and yet he was not demanding that his fate bend to his will, as lords do.

Instead, he feels balanced on the edge of his life, neither controlled, nor controlling. It must be something to do with Morgaine, he thinks.

And yet, here he is in the middle again. Neither recklessly charging forward, nor fleeing in panic. He is just there.

## Section 108

The Leth warriors charge up toward the chamber where the beast is, glowering at Vanye as they come.

The beast leaps to its feet and charges outside its chamber, where the men of Leth are.

Vanye steps back. The monster happily lets him go, and wades into the Leth warriors, splintering bodies and revelling in the carnage. The warriors quickly forget Vanye as the beast decimates their numbers.

Feeling quite well balanced on his fate, Vanye strolls through the creature's lair, takes a burning stick from its fire, and enters the tunnel on the opposite side of the chamber.

He walks down another narrow passage, his way now lit by the burning wood. Soon the sounds of the slaughter behind him fade and die.

He does not walk long before the passage starts sloping upwards again. It soon becomes so steep he is forced to climb. He carefully places his burning stick on the ground, and begins to climb.

His climb leads him out of the dank tunnel, and into the open air.

He sees fewer than ten Leth warriors and they are some sixty feet away. They have built a bonfire, and are busy shouting down the well to their comrades. Lorn is pacing angrily.

Still feeling good, Vanye moves over to the warriors' horses. He chooses Lorn's sleek black Chya horse over the scruffy Leth-bred horses.

He mounts it, and rides out of Old Ra-koris. On the journey back to new Ra-koris, he discovers Morgaine's sword Changeling fastened among the horse's saddlebags.

*Turn to section 71.*

# * **109** *

With a whispered sigh, Vanye creeps back down along the cavern. He dares not approach the beast, for fear of waking it. He has to leave it as quickly as possible. He hurries along the dark passage. He cannot see his way, but he remembers it well. He is surprised at how fast he can move through the familiar territory. Soon he is nearly at the well opening.

Ahead he sees light pouring in from the opening in the passage. He can see the wall of the well across from the opening. Distorted voices float from above and below. "There's no way he could have opened it, sir. It's an iron grate!" from below, and "Keep looking! He didn't just vanish!" from above.

Vanye breathes a sigh of relief. They have not yet discovered the hole he had crawled into. But they would not miss it forever. He looks ahead and sees ropes dangling into the pit.

He has no wish to wait for the Leth warriors to rush him in a closed corridor. The noise will surely awaken the beast, and he will be caught between two overwhelming foes.

Tensing his muscles, he leaps out into the well

shaft, grabs the rope, and hauls himself up, pulling with all his strength.

One of the Leth warriors at the bottom of the well looks up and says, "Hey . . ." in tones of helplessness and disbelief.

Vanye is out of the well in a flash, and has knocked over two of the Leth warriors before they notice him in the light of the bonfire that blazes near the well. "It's him!" one shouts. Vanye kicks the man over before he can pull out a weapon.

Leaping jagged rocks, Vanye runs across the field. A circle of six warriors closes in front of him, cutting off his escape. He pauses for a moment, bracing himself for the final conflict.

The warriors attack, clubbing him almost gently. He takes two of them out before he is beaten into unconsciousness.

*Turn to section 31.*

# * **110** *

The hard tread of boots on packed earth sounds through the cramped cavern. Vanye feels a knot in his stomach. The sight of the loathesome creature frightens him, but the thought of the sorcerous fate in store for him above frightens him more.

Vanye leaps to his feet, drawing his sword in one continuous motion. He dashes across the field of skulls, scattering brittle bone shards as he goes. He is upon the creature just as it rolls over.

Fending off Vanye's onslaught, it leaps to its feet. It snarls, foam dripping from its massive jaws. The stench of its fur is nauseating.

Just after Vanye has begun fighting the beast, the Leth warriors spill into the chamber, carrying torches. The men in front stop in their tracks, causing the ones behind to crash into them.

They back up in a fast, disorderly retreat, and watch Vanye fight the beast.

They argue quietly over whether they should intrude on the fight. They decide to move further back the way they had come, so they will have a head start running if the monster wins.

They do not bother to formulate a plan in case Vanye wins.

## PIT MONSTER

*To Hit Vanye: 10   To be hit: 12   Hit points: 20*
*Damage with claws:   Damage with longsword:*
*2 D6+2                2 D6*
                      *Damage with dagger:*
                      *1 D6*

*The Pit Monster is cunning and strong, but not fast. In addition to doing damage, its first hit will cause the monster to hold Vanye and keep him from escaping. If Vanye should try to dislodge the creature's grip on his leg, roll 3 D6 against Vanye's Strength. If the roll is less than or equal to Vanye's Strength, Vanye has freed his leg. If the roll is greater than Vanye's Strength, he is held firmly. Vanye cannot attack in the same round he is trying to free his leg.*

*If Vanye kills the Pit Monster, turn to section 100.*

*If Vanye is killed by the Pit Monster, turn to section 29.*

*If Vanye is able to get loose and decides to flee, turn to section 103. The creature gets one last attack while Vanye runs. (Note that Vanye cannot flee while his foot is held.)*

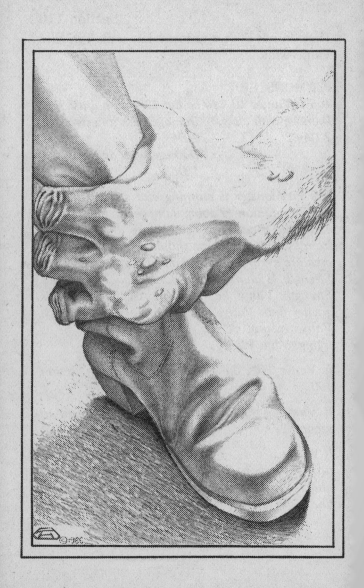